MW00528139

BRUTAL BEASTS

Craig Buchner

NFB Publishing
Buffalo, NY

Praise for *Brutal Beasts*

Craig Buchner's debut collection of stories, *Brutal Beasts*, offers us characters that are human and enchanting. I loved these stories. Poetic, voice-driven, and elegant, this book deserves placement somewhere between Kafka and Donald Barthelme, on the Dark Comedy shelf. Kudos all around.

George Singleton, author of *You Want More: Selected Stories*

These stories come at you hard, dark and disturbing (and at times hilarious) visions delivered with glittering bursts of language. Buchner's characters are often outcasts and losers, but he never allows the reader to lose sight of their humanity as they reveal the wreckage in their hearts.

Ron Rash, author of *Serena*

Startling at every turn, gorgeously written, grotesquely realistic, soulful as hell, and righteously funny, *Brutal Beasts* is a jovial mix of magic and mayhem. Transgressive, nimble, and quick-witted, Buchner's stories keep us transfixed on characters made animal by loss—of family, of friends, of a future anyone can believe in. There are monsters in these pages, but behind every horror is a heart longing for love...and a question: In a cataclysmic world defined by violence and cruelty, how far will we go to make sense of our lives?

Kim Barnes, author of *In the Kingdom of Men*

Craig's unique voice is undeniable as he shape-shifts through his carefully created worlds. The characters explore their desires, fears, and relationships in a captivating and engaging manner that demands the reader to turn the page. There is a sadness mingled with joy within the stories, encapsulating both the mundanity and unpredictability of life. I recommend *Brutal Beasts* for anyone who wants to lose themselves in the lives of others, to look through the windows of the houses of strangers, to get a glimpse of another world.

Jerry Sampson, editor of *Buckman Journal*

North Carolina fiction writer and poet Buchner's dazzling assortment of 18 tales offers a diverse cast struggling with some outlandish situations, both earthly and otherworldly… One of the assortment's greatest assets is its sublime unpredictability… The book crosses boundaries and traverses genres with seamless ease… Buchner's literary talents are on brilliant display... There is indeed mild, sunlit horror embedded in Buchner's stories, but he also demonstrates a deep understanding of human nature and how it operates in times of desperation and when faced with the paranormal.

Kirkus Reviews (Starred Review)

Cover Art by Michael Reeder

NFB
NFB Publishing/Amelia Press
119 Dorchester Road
Buffalo, New York 14213

For more information visit Nfbpublishing.com

For Alexis

TABLE OF CONTENTS

MADE BY BRUTAL BEASTS

GRABBING THE PREGNANCY test by the wrong end. First a solid pink line and a second coming into view. Kitchen shades half drawn. Light enough to see the future. But Wendy, walking into the living room, said nothing.

"This is exciting," I said. "We're excited. Right?"

I poured vodka into two tumblers. I liked good vodka; we only had bad vodka.

"Honeybear?"

Wendy didn't have the impulse to celebrate, so I poured hers down the drain. In a couple weeks, our baby would be the size of a sweet pea. It was better Wendy didn't drink.

NEW Year's Eve at the Blue House Rooftop Lodge. Our babymoon. At the last minute, my brother Ed said he'd pay the tab if he could join us.

Decoration codfish—made of Portuguese porcelain—hung on the walls; the balcony overlooked downtown.

Wendy was almost in her second trimester, and Ed asked about her nerves.

"She gets a cramp," I said, "and the next thing I know, she's on her phone reading about somebody's miscarriage."

"That's good though, right?" Ed asked. "Everything's already happened to someone so there's no surprises."

I said, "What's good if everything you read ends in miscarriage?"

"What's good is right," he said, as if it was one for the ages. But he was drunk.

Two bottles of white wine and two bottles of vodka, empty. We weren't alcoholics. But we were on vacation, and we drank like we were the real deal. If I knew the thing I'd become, maybe I'd have quit cold turkey.

"I should check on her," I said.

Wendy watched Netflix on her iPad. Binging a show about a stalker who dates the woman he follows until he finds out she's sleeping with another man. Wendy had been drawn in like a wolf to raw meat. She gave me *that* look.

"What'd you read now?" I said.

"I'm worried."

Wendy pulled up her shirt. Her stomach was relatively flat, a few dark hairs sprouting around her belly button. She cupped her left tit. "See?"

From the side, it looked like an extra nipple—the size of a pea—had grown off the tip of the original.

"Is it cancer? Be honest."

Wendy was vegan, but on trips like this, she ate cheese

and eggs and poured real cow's milk into her coffee at breakfast. *You'd have to ingest straight rBST for a century to grow a third nipple*, I thought.

Wendy inspected her other tit. "Quit staring."

"I barely looked."

I grew up Roman Catholic. When I was little, my grandmother told me all Christians were good people. And she said to always be a good boy and always tell the truth. Now that we were having our own kid, I wanted to teach it about faith. It was the practical thing to do. That was why we chose Buddhism. It was like Christianity without all the bad stuff, I had joked, but I had no idea. I only had enough of an understanding of Buddhism under my belt to know I should choose a meditation mantra—*I always have a chance to do good, I always have a chance to do right*—and that repeating it throughout the day helped clear my thoughts.

"It's probably just a skin tag," I said, staying positive. "But even if it is a nipple, you can get it removed."

Wendy wasn't listening. She squeezed the skin between her fingers, and the end bulged bright and red.

"Don't milk it," I said. "It'll pop."

"I'm sure someone on the Internet's grown a third nipple. But now you're going to say, 'if you look hard enough, you can find anything on there.' And I'm going to say, 'that means I'm right.' And you're going to get mad at me again."

I took her face between my hands. "I would never," I said, and kissed her right eyelid.

"Then you'll be annoyed," she said, looking at me with one closed eye.

"Getting warmer."

I didn't tell Ed about the third nipple. Instead I told him she was feeling better, and he poured two more drinks to celebrate.

"To the tiny victories," he said, holding up his glass.

"*Kanpai,*" I said, and clinked my glass against his.

Tomorrow we might have all the answers to life's questions, but tonight we stayed awake past midnight and watched the fireworks from the balcony, content with all we didn't know. A brocade crown filled the air with big hanging breaks of gold, slowly fading to right us. But beautiful things never last.

WORK was impossible. I spent my days at the corporate headquarters of the country's largest child care company. Elevator doors boasted vibrant images of blissful boys and girls and theys, their hands coated in bright paint and glitter, and happy teachers teaching. An invention of childhood straight from the minds of mostly single, childless marketing managers.

Similarly, I had never liked kids enough to want my own—until now.

Wendy texted during a sales meeting. She wrote, *Don't judge me.*

I held my phone beneath the conference table so only I could see the screen. *Why?*

Can you get chicken strips on your way home?

Who does vegan strips? I nodded at the Head of Marketing, who carried on about his editorial calendar. He, like the rest of us, did not have children. But we all spoke as if we knew exactly what parents needed in a child care provider.

I mean original strips. I had this memory today and now I want chicken. You don't know what it's like being pregnant.

I thought of my mantra, but between the meeting and the texting, I couldn't concentrate. I snapped off a quick reply. *What about the shitty diseases you say I'll get from real meat?*

The doctor said to listen to my body. So...

Everyone in the room nodded; I nodded along with them. *Did you Google it first?*

Fuck right off.

I stood in line at Burger King. I loved chicken tenders as a kid, but as an adult, I watched a documentary about how they were made. Lab-created super chickens with mammoth bodies, like gargantuan dogs really, except with sixteen sets of wings and no heads. Life was a horror movie, but only if you looked for it.

I'd heard women had worse cravings, but I was the accomplice to this one. Wendy didn't need authentic chicken fingers, and we knew it. They say pregnancy brain is a real thing, and this was another case of all those chemicals blasting through her body. A better plan, I told myself, was to pick up a sweet potato bowl with extra avocado from a food cart. I stepped out of line but knocked into him—the CEO at my company. Duane Everett Earp.

"Sir," I said. "I work for you. On the twelfth floor. I recognize you from your photo."

"Well, howdy," Duane Everett Earp said. He stood a few inches shorter, but he was built like an MMA flyweight. Arms striped with thin muscles and thick veins. I'd never seen him without his sport jacket.

"Are you here for dinner?" I asked.

"I'll tell you what, my wife can run circles around half the chefs in this town, but when I need comfort food, I come here. Honest to god. I can remember eating the French fries in the backseat of my momma's station wagon. Just the smell brings her back."

"I've got the same memory," I lied. "But chicken tenders. They're for my wife. Pregnancy craving."

"Expecting? You work at the right company for that, and I'll tell you, businesses like this one here inspire me," he said. "We grow up and get big-kid jobs, but there's something about this food we can't outgrow."

"I'd say you have more than a big-kid job." I didn't know what else to say.

"Looks like you're up, partner."

I ordered Wendy's chicken tenders and large fries.

Duane Everett Earp ran a two-billion-dollar business, and I was in therapy because I drank too much. But here we were, occupying the same space. The clerk pulled boxes of hot fast food from the warming tray. I looked beyond her to the French fry bin. Thousands of perfectly cut fries glowing golden under a heat lamp with white salt reflecting like diamond powder.

The cashier handed me my bag, but Duane Everett Earp stopped me.

"Do you mind? I haven't had one of their fingers in eons."

"You want one of my wife's fingers?" I asked.

"If it's not a bother."

Duane Everett Earp reached into the bag and pulled out the box, choosing one delicately fried chicken tender. His large white teeth sliced through the meat, and he pushed the rest between his pink lips, sucking off the fry and yellow grease. A red pain boiled in my gut. He licked the corner of his lips. Slick tongue lingering.

"Nothing beats a freebie," he said.

I could not remember the mantra. Screw the mantra. I had the urge to bite his neck. Let his loose body fall like a sack of old meat. There was something primal inside me.

OUR home changed. Baby stroller, baby books, car seat, and toys. We baby-proofed all the cabinet doors in the kitchen with baby blue latches, and Wendy's torpedo belly rubbed the counter as she reached for a water glass.

"How you doing? I mean, your body. You okay?"

"Never not tired," she said, panting slightly. "I never thought it would be easy, but I had no idea what it meant to have a body until now. Just moving takes effort."

"I can imagine," I said, but I couldn't. "Let's take a load off. Want to nap?"

We got into bed, and I rubbed a circular pattern on her belly, kissed the top of the mound, and then kissed her navel, then her underwear. Her crotch smelled of urine; I didn't care. Tiny hairs poked through the weave, like the flesh of a baby cactus.

I closed my eyes and listened. Inhaled and listened. Cheek nuzzled into her thigh; I could take that nap, but I kissed the cotton, and she let out the smallest moan. I kissed the inner band. Dark, thick hair flaring from beneath. Playfully I deployed to her thigh, but the hair continued.

So *furry*, I thought, and she said, "Don't stop."

But I did. Short patches of brown hair on each leg—like tufts from the belly of a wild boar. How had I not noticed? I tried to focus. The fabric and the orgasmic spots. But the hair on her thighs tickled my neck, and I got a strand in my mouth, pulling it from my lips.

"What's wrong?" Wendy stared down her chest.

Peering up between her legs, I said, "What do you mean?"

"You stopped. Keep going."

"Okay," I said. "I'm just breathing."

She laid back and said, "You can fuck me if you want to."

I said, "Maybe that's better," yanking more tangles of hair from my mouth.

Wendy rolled onto her hip, but I was soft, and it was hard to get started. She tugged my face to her tit.

"What's that?"

She said, "It's just a skin tag."

But another strip of fur like a half-moon had grown across the top of her belly. Dark and bushy. I couldn't help but think of my own body hair. Like tendrils. The pubes and the thigh and calf and butt hair I shed every time I sat on the toilet or showered or slept without underwear. Hairs lost to the most intimate spaces. She had always been different. Smooth and clean. Elevated beyond my own beastliness. But now this.

"Is that normal?" I asked.

"Do you want to Google it?" she said, smirking.

"I'm serious."

"Nothing will happen to the baby, I promise."

"Why would your hair hurt the baby?"

"What hair? I'm talking about your dick. Is that what you're worried about? Body hair?"

"Wendy," I said, and reached for her hand. Her delicate, smooth hands—all that remained hairless. "I was just saying there's a lot of it, and I wasn't sure if that's normal or not."

"I think I want to stop," she said.

"I'm sorry," I said. "I just didn't know if you knew."

"It's my fucking body, Homer. Of course I know."

I searched online for the cause. Women in forums wrote about their own experiences, the rapid hair growth. The hair usually fell out after birth. I thought of Wendy in bed. Sleeping now. Her cheek on her pillow. Her belly, the skin taut, and roots at the bottom of every single hair follicle. Blood feeding each one of them, and every single hair sprouting like a single blade of grass. All that hair pushing up through her skin breaking the surface to jacket her entire belly and arms and back. A dark, dense hide. Wendy's fur. It seemed unimaginable.

TRIVIA night at the Basement Pub meant sitting through an hour of impossible questions. It was the same gang as always: Me, Sandowski, and Gary. But this week, we let two college kids join *Bling Kong Lives*. We never won the twenty-five-dollar voucher, but we put on like we did. The college kids looked at us with admiration, but after a few wrong answers, they left the bar.

"Millennials can't commit to shit," Gary said.

"Not like us," Sandowski said.

I said, "You both have kids. How hairy did your wives get during pregnancy?"

"What do you mean hairy?" Gary asked.

I wish I'd said something funny to change the subject, but I didn't want to make things weird.

"Body hair," I said. "Like thick body hair."

Gary and Sandowski looked at one another.

"You mean 'cause she can't see where she's shaving with her belly and all?" Gary asked, and Sandowski said, "Hair in the usual spots, I guess. Like Gary said."

"Like fur. I wouldn't say it's gross, but I just wasn't sure what's normal, and you know, what's abnormal."

Gary said, "What do you mean fur? Fur, like a pelt?"

"Sure," I said.

"A pelt of what?" Sandowski asked. "You mean pelt, like p.e.l.t? Like the definition of pelt, pelt?"

They had both been married for over ten years, so maybe I was thinking of things the wrong way. Or maybe they forgot on purpose.

"Forget it," I said.

"I'm not sure I can," Sandowski said.

"Next round's definitely on you, Homer."

IT did not end with chicken strips. The week after, Wendy wanted corn dogs, and then hamburgers. Animalistic urges.

Naked, Wendy stared at her laptop, pillows propping her up in bed. She reached for a handful of fries from a greasy bag and wedged them into her mouth. One landed on the sheets.

"Napkin?" I asked.

"Starving," she grunted.

Months earlier she would've crucified me for spilling food, but I returned to her with a plate.

"You uncomfortable?"

"Overheating," she grunted.

Her large breasts hung over her enormous belly, with our baby's legs and arms swiping within. Nipples poking out new tufts of hair. Her entire stomach now covered in fur, armpit hair flaring from the creases. All of it somehow seemed unnatural. But like a mother chimpanzee, she sat naked and hairy, and she hand-picked crumbs from her own body.

"You're making a mess," I said.

She looked at me, the same foul stare I got when I drank too much, but she didn't speak. Instead, a rumble escaped her body.

THPPTPHTPHPHHPH.

This squealing flatulence sliced through any other distraction. Yet, she held my gaze.

"Did you just... fart?" I asked.

"Fell out," she said, slow and thick, like she spoke the words through water.

When she finished, she quickly fell asleep. Around her snoring, I cleaned the discarded wrappers and pulled the blanket all the way up to the sprouts of hair on her jawline. I kissed her singular eyebrow, and she snorted. Dreaming, her arms and legs flinched, as if in chase. I had no idea of what, so I imagined all the possibilities. A jackal charging down a rabbit. A horse breaking across a field. A tiger leaping for a gazelle. A dog fetching a limp pheasant. Maybe even Wendy, black coat of fur bristling, racing on all fours after a feral cat, its terrified yellow eyes swelling as Wendy snapped her mighty jaws into its weak, poor body. The crack of bone at the end. But then she stopped. Arms and legs were now motionless in sleep. Silence was her perfection.

THE idea of failure was something I talked about weekly with Monirée, my therapist. I didn't know much about Monirée except her office was too dark because the 20-watt bulb in the lamp in the corner was always failing.

In her quiet "trust-me" voice, she said, "Tell me about your week, Homer. Don't leave anything out."

I set my palm against my chin, like I was giving it incredible thought.

"Great week," I said.

"Good." Her eyebrows bounced. "And your job?"

"Great."

"Positive," Monirée said. "And your drinking?"

"Dry as a bone," I said, which was mostly true now that Wendy's due date was closing in. "Living the best version of me."

"Your eyes look red," she said, then nodded as if to confirm. "Did you say you have allergies?"

I said, "Not much sleep with Wendy peeing all night. Everything pushes on her bladder."

Monirée wrote something in her notepad, but only said, "And how's that?"

I reached my arms over my head. I wasn't stretching; I didn't know what to do with my hands. We looked into one another's eyes. I looked away because I was doing it again, thinking I failed before I started.

"How is 'us'?" I asked.

"If that's what you want to talk about."

"We're changing. But it's good."

She didn't jot anything down; she didn't nod; she just said, "Changing how?"

"How we communicate. That stuff."

Monirée smiled. "Is that it? You had a great week at work, you're not drinking, and things are good with your wife?"

It wasn't *it*. I could go on all session dodging her, or I could just tell her.

I said, "I'm getting hung up on how Wendy looks, but I think that's normal. Is that normal?"

"It's a lot to take in," she said, "with a baby growing inside of her. Do you feel left out?"

I said, "I don't do much, you know, in terms of helping the baby right now. So, yeah, maybe I feel like my job's over."

"But your next job is beginning. And she'll need to feel like you're committed, right? Not just to her but to both of them."

"But what about the hair?" I asked. "I think we're getting off topic."

It took me an hour to bring it up, but I knew our session was almost over. I wanted to talk about it, or I'd drown the problem back down inside me.

"What hair?"

"The pelt," I said. "Her entire body. Is that normal for pregnant women?"

"I'm not really sure. I'd assume some hair growth would be normal, considering everything she's going through." Then she asked, "Did you Google it?"

WEEKS leading up to the delivery, we talked in grunts and groans and mumbles and snorts. The toilet and bathtub were covered in her hair, and I vacuumed the living room daily. Piles of loose hair everywhere. Wendy slept fourteen and sixteen hours a day, and when she woke, she would wait at the back door until I opened it for her. She paced for a few minutes in the backyard, coming back inside panting.

"You feeling okay?"

"Uh."

Wendy drank water straight from the faucet, then got back into bed.

The Internet did not help, and the mantra could not bring us back.

LAST New Year's Eve on the rooftop deck, Ed and I traded stories of childhood. After midnight and firecracker-drunk, we remembered winter days without power, remembered all the lamps our mother had bought after the divorce, remembered the hole in the station wagon floor that let us see the world beneath our feet as we drove, like we were princes on a flying carpet.

Ed said, "I used to have a cash cup in my room."

"From when you worked at Subway?"

"Mom would steal money out of it to pay her credit card bills. I had a hundred IOUs."

I closed my eyes, and I could see that claustrophobic house on the corner of Middle Line Road. Unfinished sheet rock walls. Cracked lamp shades. Empty cupboards. The stack of orange and yellow notices on the kitchen table like they were party napkins.

We stood against the railing. "Too bad Subway didn't pay more," I said, and elbowed him. "So you're to blame we grew up poor?"

The fireworks finale had ended long ago, but every so often, an orphan shot streamed across the night. A blood-shot pop and blue gasp of smoke. From the terrace, we looked over the city and smirked at something far away. In the distance or the past. Maybe we had escaped.

"In a fucked-up way, you're not wrong," Ed said. "Now drink up while you got it. Because you'll be on baby watch soon enough."

A car drove into the alleyway below us. There was only enough room to drive in and reverse out, but the car tried to turn around. A ten-point turn until it was stuck. The driver opened the door and inspected any clearance he still might have. He lit a cigarette, and then he walked away. Someplace was more important than this problem.

"Could you ever leave?" I asked. The retreating man had no idea what was ahead of him in the alley, but he headed straight into the shadows. "Like Dad?"

"That's why I don't want kids."

"Why's that?"

Ed said, "So I don't have to find out."

WENDY nested in bed with a body pillow clutched between her legs. Going on sixteen hours of sleep. I posted up in the living room. The baby could come any day. I wondered what that day would be like. A stranger in our family. We had no idea who we were getting. We had all the information about everything we could ever need, yet tiny limbs of fear crawled over my skin. I needed levity, but I was on strict sobriety. A glass of ice-cold water to ground me into the present.

I watched *Animal Planet*, a show about dogs. A golden retriever named Lulu padded around a bed on a square of newspapers. Her belly sagged, nipples red and protruding. I don't remember if I fell asleep or not, but I remember seeing Wendy's sad eyes, like Lulu's, then waking to her yelling from the room. *Labor*, I thought. She sat straight up in bed, grabbing at her thighs. It seemed like it happened so fast. But I had a chance to do right.

"What is it? Tell me what's wrong."

Her speech was thick and sloppy. "My leg," she groaned.

"Did your water break? Should I look it up?"

For nine months they were together, mother and pas-senger. And though I had done my part in the beginning, I was back again.

"Cramp," she said.

"What?"

"M'okay."

"Are you okay? Did you say you're okay?"

"Cramp. Leave."

I did not go back to sleep. I laid in the dark beside her, listening to her breath. Our child was under the surface of her skin. Waiting for its moment. Waiting to grow and learn and have its own mantra. Waiting to love us, hate us, run from us, and fly back to us. All of its life swept through my head. That was my trial.

EVEN the real thing flashed by. The drive to the hospital. The nurses. Our doctor. Twenty hours.

In the delivery room, I can remember her legs covered in sweat. All of the furniture was another shade of blue, except the pine veneer cabinets. The doctor wore circular glasses like John Lennon, and Wendy was moaning and crying, and someone—a nurse—calmly, slowly said, "Now." A tiny cone-shaped head emerging from her, glazed in gore. I cut the cord.

Wendy nuzzled the child. The waste from her own body on its head. Not human, but alive. The smell of new birth. Wild-haired and unruly. They were skin to skin in the bed, and I stood only a few feet away, but the gap looked like a million, million miles through my eyes. There was one future that would never begin for me, and this was the new future. I knew I needed to get to them, but we had been so distant. Speaking entirely different languages. One human, one animal. A moment of rage stopped me. Red spots blurring the curves of sight, and I saw her, our child—a daughter. Pale and wrinkled, she was frantic until Wendy showed her love; she licked her forehead. Forget all the hair and gore, it was kindness. It was pure. And I needed that; I needed *her*.

The room was the dark night in that dark alley, and I was that stranger walking into the shadows. I could not see into the unknown, and I was afraid, but a crying joy replaced that fear—this was nature's revelation. The way Wendy's fingers traced her face. I wanted everything between them. They brought me to my knees, as if in prayer. If they asked me, I would kill for them and then lick their perfect heads clean.

HOME, SOMEWHERE

MY BROTHER STARED at his pigs. 10 a.m., Christmas morning. He leaned against the wooden pigpen. Twenty-two ounce can of Twisted Tea in hand, two empties at foot. We stood in an inch and a half of fresh snow like there wasn't mud underneath. I mirrored him. Same leg back, same hand wrapped around the railing, watching the pigs chew cobs of corn. Grunting. I spit, almost hitting a hoof. I spit again but missed all together.

"Missed breakfast," I said, handing Josh a card. "Dad had this for you. Said he had a photo album too."

Josh said, "I'm not taking nothing."

"Least fifty bucks," I said, but pocketed the card.

Josh ripped another can from the plastic six-pack yoke. "You want?"

Shadow-bellied clouds muddied the sky. It could snow again or rain. Either way, it wouldn't be good weather.

Earlier that morning, I heard my father say what he says most: "Near record highs and, bam, it's freezing nuts when I get out of bed." Always something about the weather; that hadn't changed. "All them reports saying global warming. It's you kids wanted everything plastic," he went on. He never let us starve, but he had his theories over the years. No cars from Japan because they would explode and kill us, 9/11 was a blood offering, and *they're all* looking deep into us through our own computers.

It was Dad's third Christmas without Mom. I don't know why I brought him up to Josh, but I haven't seen Josh mad in a while, not since the last time I was here. When we were young, Josh was always knock-your-teeth-out mad. But I never hated him.

"Don't owe him a thing," Josh said.

He cracked another can, twisted off the tab. A short guzzle followed.

"I can't believe he let you take Ma's ride," Josh said.

"Said he needed the truck."

The pigs ran from the muddy rink to the shelter, popping in and out of the cutout wall. I had my own sixer of Busch on the passenger seat of Ma's car, but I grabbed a can of Twisted Tea, poured a lap into the mud. Two pigs charged, diving snout-deep through the snow, chomping at the tea-mud. Ma had left for Florida. Got on a plane and was gone, no forwarding address. She said the cold hurt her bones, but we knew it was Dad's drinking.

"Fired Ron," Josh said.

I looked at his house across the yard. Green algae covering blue siding, a blue like some view dissolving in the distance.

I said, "Today?"

"Yep," he said.

"Good Christ," I said, half-impressed. I'd met Ron once. A family man. Good father. Good-looking too, for his age.

Old black shutters framed the new windows, the ones Ron had installed, though one shutter had fallen off. Underneath, a history of the house before my father sold it to my brother, an immature blue siding the same as when my mother and father owned it, when I was only five years old. A new-beginning blue.

My father was twenty-eight when he sided the house, one year older than my mother. Dad hung the sheets by hand, hammer dangling from his belt. Shirt off, bronze summer skin. Mustache still muddy brown. And my mother watched him dreaming of some life she never got. The blue of something that could've been but wasn't.

"Only day I can watch Ron do it the way I want," Josh said. "But hired him right back, and he says he'll be here after his kids wake up. I told him whenever's just fine."

I said, "That's an asshole move. Something Dad would do."

"You're the asshole," Josh said, thinking—I bet—that I was kidding.

I said, "You can't let nobody be happy. Probably the only day of the year he gets a blowjob." And for a moment, I let myself picture it.

"Watching the pigs," Josh said, "and drinking are about the only things you need to be happy."

I said, "I'm heading down to Gram's. You coming?"

"Told her I was working all day."

The men in our family worked holidays, whether they left the house or not. If their construction site was closed, they started in on an unfinished bedroom or the basement. No one argued, so they worked often.

Josh dropped his empty Twisted Tea into the pigpen, pigs rushing to chomp the metal. He pulled another can from the yoke.

He said, "Going to finish up here."

COMING home to Perth, New York, was like wandering into a bad memory. The town was old, houses small and decrepit. In Ma's hatchback, I drove the old roads from my childhood. Midline Road. Voorhees Road. Highway 30. It had been years since I'd seen the roller-skating rink, *High Rollers*, or the junkyard across from it. I thought of my first kiss as a fifth grader at the rink. A girl named Alyssa dared me to kiss my best friend Kevin, and we said fuck you, we're not gay. But in the bathroom, Kevin said it wasn't a big deal, and I let him stick his tongue in my mouth.

We weren't as afraid after that. We were telling each other we were naked in his bed to prepare us for a time when there was a girl. We rubbed our bodies against one another until we were bored, and then we stole his mother's Parliaments and acted wild in the world. In the junkyard, we would swing crowbars against cars, pound dents in the doors, shatter headlights, and run like mad when we heard the watchdog barking. But that thrill paled in comparison to the first time we fucked.

It was raining now, and the windshield was fogged. The defrost knob maxed, I drank a can of Busch, passing the trailer park where my parents lived before I was born. Even when we lived in the old house, I had no idea everyone wasn't poor.

I wiped the windshield with my sleeve and saw a blur on the road. I swerved. My foot clamped on the brake. The car slid, slamming into the gutter. A mailbox punched the windshield, the seatbelt locked across my chest, and I kissed the horn cap, splitting my lip.

I checked the mirrors and shifted into reverse, wheels spinning, shifting back and forth, but nothing. I opened the door, and I climbed out of the ditch—the road was empty.

Someone behind me was calling. From the top of the driveway, a man yelled down from his porch. He was dressed in red pajamas.

"It's okay," I said. "I'm okay."

The man said, "You better have insurance, or I swear."

"I'll pay for it," I said. "I got cash."

"Cash? Come on up," he said. "Don't have my shoes on."

The man said his name was Leroy Kilpatrick. He sat in the La-Z-Boy near the window, rain beads patting the glass. Tufts of gray fur were balled in the creases of his pajamas. The odor inside the house was raw meat.

"What do you think it would cost?" I asked.

"That old box cost me eighty bucks at Lowe's," Leroy said.

"My brother can tow me," I said, counting out fifty dollars—Christmas cash—from my wallet, then opened Josh's card and offered Leroy fifty more.

Leroy folded the bills in half. "I guess I don't see no need to call the authorities about this," he said, handing me the cordless phone.

When my brother answered, I said, "I know you been drinking, but I need a tow."

"Call Dad," he said.

"Funny," I said. "He wouldn't even bail me out the last time."

I wrapped the chains around Josh's hitch and the bumper of the car. The grill had buckled, and the wheel wells were tucked back. Josh's truck rocked forward, the chain tightening, and the car bucked, crawling out of the ditch.

"People got to be careful on this road," Leroy said.

I said, "Thought I saw a dog in the road."

"It's that Stuben boy playing tricks."

"I went to school with a Ricky Stuben."

"Hit by a car. About where yours is," Leroy said. "The ghost of Richard Stuben."

"That's not funny," I said.

Josh adjusted the chains. "Guess I'm going to Gram's," he yelled, chomping gum. Always, like Dad, after a few drinks.

"Watch out for ghosts," Leroy said, waving goodbye.

GRANDMA Jean sat at her table buttering a slice of rye bread before adding a second layer. We were an hour and a half late for lunch, but family was always late. Her AM radio played. Call-ins about the new Super Walmart.

"Your brother put on so much weight," Grandma Jean said. "You should talk to him. He never listens to me."

Josh shook his head, and I scooped goulash from the casserole dish.

"I'm sitting right here," Josh said.

As a kid, I would egg Josh on just to get a rise out of him. I figured this out at group talk. It was all about power, but I was getting too old for such antics, so I kept my mouth shut.

"I just worry about you two," Grandma Jean said. "It's a shame neither of you can settle down. Have your own families."

"It's this place," I said, and squirted ketchup on the goulash. I thought about my boyfriend Chris back in Oregon. "There's no one here for everybody, if I'm being honest."

"And the West Coast is so much different?" Josh said.

"I'm dating regular," I said.

"And who's this?" Gram asked. "A nice Polish girl?"

Even though I knew talk was good, being honest never came easy.

"No," I said. "Not Polish."

"You think someone from the outside could handle this place?" Josh asked. "You got another thing coming, man. When you going to tell the truth?"

They wouldn't understand.

"I heard Ricky Stuben died in a car accident," I said.

Ricky was a few years younger, and I met him a dozen times in high school, but I always pretended I didn't know him. I had no idea why, but I can't apologize now.

"I'm trying to talk to you," Josh said to me. "Don't get me mad."

"Who died?" Grandma Jean asked.

I said, "Near the old chicken store."

Grandma Jean said, "I remember. He was standing in the middle of the road."

"He was not," Josh said. "He was walking on the wrong side and a car clipped him. Driver probably thought he was a deer. Died in the gutter. That's what the paper said."

"I can't wait to die," Grandma Jean said.

I said to Josh, "You won't give nobody a fair shake."

Josh said, "I can't deal with this absolute negativity." He went to the refrigerator. "Don't you got nothing but Coors, Gram?"

"It's gluten-free," she said. "The doctor says I need to watch that."

"No, it isn't," Josh said. "Everything's got glutens."

"That's why I don't talk to him," she said. "He never listens."

"You should've drank more or started smoking," he said, sitting at the table again. "It's your own fault you're still alive."

"Goulash is real good," I said.

"Nobody ever listens to me," she said. "This is what I'm talking about."

Josh nodded at me. "Time to go?" he asked, then he said

to Grandma Jean, "I'll swing by tomorrow and knock your icicles down. They're big enough to kill a man."

"You were always a good boy," Grandma Jean said. "I used to think you'd be a priest. Maybe someday?"

I kissed her cheek. She smelled the same as she did two years ago and ten years ago and more—floral and soft. She'd smell the same, I'm sure, at her wake.

TREES lined Dad's long, winding driveway, leafless maple branches hanging overhead. Josh towed Ma's car as I steered. He stopped halfway down the driveway, and I helped pull the chains off.

I said, "You coming in? Dad's got that photo album."

"Nah," he said. "I can see him whenever."

I said, "First you don't have time for Gram. But you're here now."

"You think everything's so easy. Like there's some perfect goodness, and fate just happens to work out the way you want, huh?" he said. "Why do you even come back if you hate it so much?"

I could see my father's trailer through the naked trees. Most of the morning snow had melted, the ground patchy with dark muddy moats, swampy leaves. Our father stood on the porch.

"If that's Josh," Dad yelled, "tell him to hold on."

"Don't you want more than this?" I asked.

Josh said, "You think you're better than it all."

"I got pictures for him," Dad said, ambling off the porch.

I asked Josh, "Are you happy here?"

27

"I'm not hiding," he said. "You follow me? If we're being honest with one another, I'm not the one with any secrets."

"You don't know what you're even talking about," I said.

Josh said, "You're not hearing me. I don't care. You're a grown man, for Christ's sake. Quit acting like a fucking baby about it."

"Fuck you," I said, because the words seemed right. Because I knew he was right.

He stepped up into his truck, the door closing hard, always the sound of slamming. "I'm not hanging around for him to lose it over Mom's car."

"What even happened here?" Dad scuffed his feet through wet snow. Chomping a stick of gum, he said, "Christ, what did I say to you before you left? Said no drinking." Then he asked Josh, "And you been drinking too?

"Are you out of your mind?" Josh asked, arm hanging out the window.

"Black ice," I said. "I'll call about getting it fixed today."

"It was an accident," Josh said. "Don't get all wound up."

Dad said, "If your mother saw. She bought this with her own money. Her car, her rules. You don't know the half of it."

"This ain't monkey talk," I said.

"Don't go nutso on me," Dad said. "Your mother drops everything and goes, and what'd I get when she left? Everything goddamn runs a' shit, is what."

It was the first time I'd ever heard him say it.

"Boozing," Josh said, red-faced. "You know why everyone goddamn runs off."

Dad said, "Don't even start about drinking because she never had a problem with me. It was the two of you always wanting. But I kept giving in. Telling her it'd get better. She couldn't take all the wanting. Christ, even as adults."

Back on the road, a town dump truck passed, plow down, metal scraping asphalt, leaving a wake of salt and sand.

I had wanted Josh to drive away instead of opening his door, trudging toward our father. I had wanted him to start over in Georgia or Florida and then visit in a year or two to tell me and Chris all about his new life, his soon-to-be fiancé, the new job and house, their family plans—thankful for the changes.

Josh stood nose-to-nose with our father. The wind picked up, and I shook. I remembered how Josh's pigs had scampered to the fence that morning after his can of Twisted Tea, their teeth grating through aluminum. A fence to keep them from the rest of the world. But like monsters they gazed up at him, gums cut from jagged metal edges. They snorted and waited—that close to happiness.

We were still only at the beginning where Mom had left us, but maybe it would end differently. And when I returned to Oregon, I would tell Chris all of this. He knew nothing of this place, even though it had made me. I would tell him the trip went the way it had to.

I said, "Let's go inside. We'll figure everything out."

Because it had to end with grace.

BABY TEETH

BECOMING A FATHER was the single most amazing thing that ever happened to me, but it had its ups and downs. In the pitch dark, windows taped over with newspapers and blankets, I sat and listened. Her tiny coos under the swell of rumbling outside. Hordes of undead who didn't know we were on the second floor. They followed our neighbor, Chester Lime, who let all those yellow-headed dandelions grow until they were white whispers floating into our yard.

We heard him yelling, pounding; we heard his fingers scrape the boarded dog door. They tore him to pieces. He was calling out, "Howie!" In a panic, he sounded like a coyote. That was what I told my wife, Reba. It was just a dog. A simple protection, that lie. Like the old days, when I believed misogynistic courtesy was a luxury.

THE next morning, I peeled back a triangle of paper from the window. I turned the flannel I had worn for a month inside out. Slid my arms back into the sleeves. A superstition from football. Never launder a jersey during a winning streak.

Reba half-nursed a half-asleep Lucy Pearl in our bed.

"I'll go out alone," I said, like an old routine: *I'll clean the gutters; I'll rake the leaves.*

"We'll come." Reba scooched herself out of bed. Slid a bowie knife into her sheath.

"You're not taking her," I said. "Make me a grocery list. Remember that? What do you want?"

Reba smirked. "Equal rights?"

"That's a blast from the past," I said. "But I won't risk her. Or you."

"You think that matters—this chivalry, or whatever it is?"

I used to look both ways in traffic for her; I used to pay for her dinner. That was part of the past I longed for. Things weren't right, but things were alive.

"I'll stay," Reba said, "for her. Not 'cause you said so."

I lumbered halfway down the stairs.

"It's too warm for that shirt," she called. "If they chase you, you'll wish you didn't wear it."

Maybe she was right. Maybe the lucky flannel wasn't lucky. Maybe it was the beard. I left the flannel bunched on the stairs.

The future is female. I had that bumper sticker on my car. Before Lucy Pearl, before all this. But now, the future was surviving. I knocked on the front door with the flat end of the splitting maul and put my ear to the wood.

"Yoo-hoo," I said. "Anybody out there?"

From the top of the stairs, Reba said, "Quiet. She just fell asleep."

"I'm opening the door."

Her voice jumped. "Follow the rules."

I checked the peephole. Saw Chester's house and the horde of a hundred thousand dandelions in the yard.

"Now I'm opening the door," I said.

The parting brought a rush of warm air that lifted the hair on my arms. Blue sky and clear roads. Even in a world of shit, beauty never died. I heard Reba on the stairs. Her rumble. I saw the panic in her face; then I saw what was left of Chester. Legless and snout down on the welcome mat.

Reba was halfway down the staircase when her feet twisted in the lucky flannel. Arms flung out to brace her fall, Lucy Pearl suspended in space. She thudded on the linoleum in the foyer inches from Chester. Reba struck the floor too. A coyote-yip of pain.

"Grab her." Reba cradled her arm.

Chester's head lifted only to snap against the floor like a rat trap. Reba scrambled for Lucy Pearl, and I drew the maul over my head. Lopped it across Chester's neck. Splitting half-way loose. Another windmill chop freed his head completely.

I can't say why I booted him, but I kicked Chester's head and it ricocheted from the wall, recoiling back into Lucy, tummy-down. One bite, and two red crescents tattooed her crown. I leapt into the air and landed heavily. Chester's jaw split. Imagine a ripe fig. Breaking all his teeth like the seeds decorating pink pulp.

STIFF muscles, excessive saliva, fever, nausea. Those were the initial symptoms. Then the spasms. We thought Lucy was going to break every bone in her body until we swaddled her.

"We need to lock her in place with leather belts."

"Babies don't need that," Reba said.

"We don't know."

"You're going to do what you're going to do."

"Yes, I am."

The metal buckles rattled all night. When her eyes lightened, a glacial blue, she was one of them. Her jaws now ever chomping.

REBA blamed herself; I blamed myself. But all the blame in the world wouldn't change Lucy back. She watched us, cried for us. But now she wanted to consume us.

Reba expressed milk into a bottle. Held it to her tiny blue lips, but Lucy wouldn't drink. She spit it up and panted until she gagged on empty breaths.

"I can't take it. She needs to nurse."

"If you release her, you're going to kill us."

"Now I'm going to do what I'm going to do."

Reba unstrapped Lucy Pearl and brought her to her tit. Tiny arms clawing at her face. Lucy's toothless maw gnawed Reba's dark nipple. Pink gums mashing Reba's skin, mouth around her areola. Milk dripped from her lips. We were never happier than tonight.

FOR two months, Reba nursed our undead girl, and I

scavenged the neighborhoods. The hordes had followed the meat to Portland and Eugene. There was no one here except us, farmland, houses, barns, and pantries. Pantries brimming with cans of red beans, ravioli, tuna fish, cranberry sauce, pinto beans, and fruit cocktail with cherries. And we had tools and gasoline and hunting rifles. There wasn't any reason we couldn't live in Shangri-La forever.

But Lucy Pearl's mouth had a problem. Reba's nipples were swollen, the skin bruised. I used my pinky to feel inside her mouth. Her once-round gums peaked.

"Did you feel this?"

"She can't break the skin."

"Are you suicidal?"

Lucy was five and a half months old. We sat in the dark and planned her future.

"What about cotton balls?" I said.

"You can't tape inside her mouth. Maybe a mouth guard."

"They don't make 'em for babies."

Reba put her face into her hands. "I'm trying my best."

I rubbed her back. "Other people have to have this problem."

She drew her hands down her face, cheeks stretched under the tension. "My mother used to tell me she'd loop a string around my tooth and tie the other end to a doorknob."

"And she'd slam the door," I finished.

"What if we just yank it out?"

THE Hyacinths bloomed in September. At dusk, the world was purple mountains. Gray barns falling in on themselves, but pink skylight snuck through holes like playful snakes.

We ate dinner on the porch: shepherd's pie with pheasant meat. Shared a bottle of Chester's Yellow Tail shiraz.

"You ever imagine this?" I said, and sipped. The wine left no legs on the glass; I couldn't help but think of Chester on our welcome mat.

"More," Reba said, gulping hers.

I missed the old world. Paying twice the worth of a bottle of wine at a restaurant. Waiting an hour in line for brunch. Those horrible half-year reviews at work.

"I've been pulling nails from a board," I said. "Practice."

Reba said, "Do you remember getting circumcised?"

We heard Lucy cry like a wild animal, and the bottle of wine was empty.

"We should do it now."

IN every world there are rites and rituals. Like smoke drifting off of censors in church for the souls they were meant to save. We lit tea candles, and Reba placed Lucy on the table, a spread of instruments before her: pliers, scissors, a needle, and thread.

"I should do it," Reba said. "It was my idea."

"I can do it." I took hold of the needle nose.

Reba set her hand on mine, restraining the pliers. "You need to stop trying to protect me."

"I know," I said, re-gripping them.

Reba guided the pliers from my hand. "I need you to stop, or we're not going to make it."

"It reminds me of back then."

"But this is now," Reba said, and she pried Lucy's lips apart with her fingers. "And you're going to stop."

I was never ready for this world. I had lived too long in the old days. I remembered too clearly. But I said, "Yes."

"Then count to three," Reba said. "But count up. I never liked it down."

Today had been like every day: morning, noon, and night. In the moment that followed, the silence began. But then it swelled.

I held Lucy Pearl, and she suckled the cold pliers. Being a father had its ups and downs. We stood in the candlelit dark, windows taped over with newspapers and blankets, as the silence grew louder and louder.

Masters of Matchsticks

THEY WERE ALL Katrinas to me. The storm. My wife. Those Chihuahuas running like mad all over town. Wrecking balls and masters of Irish goodbyes. Everybody left for Connecticut or Texas, but Rogey sat tight. Friends since before elementary school. Way back. Everything was built to last then: radios, lighters, relationships.

We sat on the porch, last bottle of whiskey between us, Rogey's BB gun slung across the railing. In the game, smoking pot was illegal because it made you shoot better. Booze was allowed, but no shithead drank whiskey and expected to hit the broadside of a barn, let alone one of the Chihuahuas named Katrina. Except me.

"See that black and white Katrina?" Rogey asked. "Little rat thing."

Hundreds of dogs ran the streets. All day. All night. Packs doubling. Tripling. Without people around, they took over. But it was worse than that.

You look out on Biloxi now, you see matchsticks. Like God shook all them houses in his hand and shot them scattering across the county into splinters. But that was nothing without the bodies. Rogey lived near Edmund's Funeral and the water washed the bodies out, like dead wood littered around the city. A man's arm wrapped over the low bars of the grated security door at Shear Krissy's Salon and Beautification School, or that water-logged woman wedged under the carriage of Zengo's taco truck, or that naked boy, Jayme Davis, in the center of the street, like he was dreaming. But the stink of formaldehyde and methanol hooked into the air, velvety across your tongue, heavy and sour, not like sweet Krispy Kreme air.

Maybe we misunderstood God in times like this. What if he reached down and grabbed up the houses and our lives too, everyone destined down some fated path? Maybe he lost a bet with the devil, but I don't pretend to understand what they would bet on. Losing like a man, he shook us like dice and threw us out again.

Rogey breathed loud and steadied the BB gun. Bunched in a pile in Mr. Gillin's yard, twenty or thirty Chihuahuas crawled over one another. Gilly's wife left the same time Katrina did. North for family. And like me, Gilly too would weather the storm.

When the skies cleared, I had found Zeiss binoculars washed up against the foundation. People suddenly wore costumes. Wet suits walking the sidewalk, orange life vests in the stores. At first, I had bragged to complete strangers.

From the porch, I called down to a man pushing a grocery cart of batteries. "*Zeus* binoculars. Says right here." I pointed at the logo on the left barrel.

"Zeiss," he said, too far to read the script. "What a waste."

I said, "No sir, I watch stray dogs."

"I know," he had said, pushing his cart away.

Rogey fired the BB gun, and the black and white Katrina jumped from the pile, struck in the heel or the thigh. Even the Zeiss couldn't tell for certain. The rest of the dogs ran too, thirty Chihuahuas scattering like cockroaches.

Mr. Gillin was flat on his belly in his yard. Half-devoured. White fat marbled through red flesh. The dogs had done a number, but they were on to another body by now.

Rogey cocked his gun, and I swallowed a slug of whiskey. *They'll be back*, I thought. I watched Rogey take aim, steady the barrel. *They always come back.* I let out a hot, red breath and narrowed my sights too, looking hard into something like the future. God and everybody knows that Biloxi means first people. We learned that in the second grade. I wondered what they'll call me and Rogey.

American Metal

My American Metal (**Blog Entry**): *December 13*

I never read much before, but here it kills time. *Band of Brothers. Catch-22. The Thin Red Line.* Most everybody watches movies. I can't take the violence on TV, but I'm excited to fire at something other than paper targets. Maybe everybody is, but no one's saying much. Guess I'm looking for insight into somebody else's experience. Just being away from home, I guess, is like every other deployment. So I lie in wait, and I read until the shooting starts.

My American Metal (**Blog Entry**): *December 28*

In our Combat Lifesaver course, I had to start a line on a guy named Dover, but he did me first. He was all shaky and massacred my arm, a lot of holes and blood. He probably thought I'd take revenge and stab him a hundred times, but I liked him okay, so I got his vein the first try. We learned how to treat gunshot wounds: check the airway, breathing, circulation, disability; then apply pressure to the wound and use pressure points to control the bleeding. The instructor stood at the front of the room. He said, "There's an eighty-goddamn-five-percent chance you will need to apply what you've learned here in the next six months." Most everybody laughed, but he was dead serious.

My American Metal (Blog Entry): *January 2*
It's a land of extremes. Streets piled with trash, and you see an old man like your grandfather yakking away on a cell phone while he's steering a cart being pulled by a donkey, then moving out of the way for a Lexus SUV with gold rims. You could drive by mud huts and then see a palace that looks like it came off the Vegas strip.

My American Metal (Blog Entry): *January 10*
The bars are in houses, like old-time speakeasies. They're set behind this 20-foot wall that goes on forever, protected by a perimeter of security guards. I met a girl named Lee Marie in the bathroom, and we made out next to some dudes pissing.

My American Metal (Blog Entry): *February 12*
At the range, we shot every kind of specialty weapon we could carry without having a tank or an aircraft. We found this little tin shack about 100 yards away, big enough to hit with most handhelds. I fired all kinds of things: AK47, M16A2, MK47, minigun, LAW, Carl Gustav, PKM, .50 Cal, 240B, SCAR heavy, Barrett sniper rifle, M4 shorty/conventional, M203, 9mm pistols, a 6-shooter semi-auto

grenade launcher. Before we left, we had to clean up the area, which meant we blew a giant hole in the ground with explosives, threw in all the garbage and shells, etc., and blew it up again with C4. On the ride back, there were the same locals watching us cruise by, some kids waving, some staring like we were from Mars.

My American Metal (Blog Entry): *February 26*
Rumor was Rainwater and Dover got caught by the MPs on the roof of our barracks. The official report said they were engaged in a "voluntary wrestling exercise." You can't talk about that shit.

My American Metal (Blog Entry): *March 13*
Finally. Got Lee Marie alone. But in bed, you can hear Apache helicopters passing overhead. No matter how hard your dick is, you never forget there's a war going on.

My American Metal (Blog Entry): *April 21*
Opium is cheaper than water. You see it on the streets: men, women, grandmas, everybody. I asked Sabir, the interpreter, why. He said the Taliban kill their families every day. "What would you do?" he asked me.

My American Metal (Blog Entry): *May 10*
A dozen light explosions at 0400. Harassment fire. Maybe RPGs. None hit inside the fence. Sometimes I think we're untouchable.

My American Metal (Blog Entry): *May 30*

In mess hall, Rainwater started up about Thailand again. He said a man-killing bull elephant slaughtered every single mercenary group that's tried to bring it down. "I'll be a fucking legend down there," he said. "I'll kill the son of a bitch." We were all getting itchy.

My American Metal (Blog Entry): *June 15*

Woke to an explosion. Scared the holy shit out of me. Dover said it was some kind of weapon sent our way but not to worry. He said if I was still scared, I could sleep with him and pretend he was Lee Marie. But Rainwater walked in. I thought he'd rip us in half, but he went for something in his lockbox and left.

My American Metal (Blog Entry): *June 23*

Another mission outside the wire. Rode in an open Hummer with a 240B pointing out the backend. I was like an action hero. We cruised through a tiny village and the kids chased us, smiling, waving. Half of them didn't have teeth. But they all had beautiful eyes.

"Sand fucker, sand fucker, sand fucker," Rainwater yelled, pointing at them, his hand like a pistol. "Bang, bang, bang."

Then he holstered his invisible sidearm and threw them a handful of breath mints.

We got to the range and fired off all the big guns, making sure everything was sighted, operating properly. We took Sabir. It was endless blue skies. Reminded me of the Palouse. I told Sabir it would've been great if we had some hard cider, but he had no idea. He just asked about New York City, and if I watched David Lettermen every night.

My American Metal (Blog Entry): *July 2*
We weren't trained for what happened. Somebody "found" opium and a Koran in Rainwater's lockbox. I figured Rainwater didn't believe in anything.

My American Metal (Blog Entry): *July 27*
Our first trip off base since the shooting. Fuck. How do you get past something like that? I keep seeing it in my head. Over and over. How does that even happen to one of your own?

The convoy drove high into the mountains. There was nothing but rocks and the single paved road cutting through the creases of the world. All the locals squatted along the road and the kids ran toward us waving like lunatics. We drove to a big open area into what used to be a Russian military camp. The building looked 50 years old. Abandoned, falling apart. There were radio towers and watchtowers. We stopped the trucks, looked around. We couldn't see another living thing for 10 miles. Looked like something out of an old movie set at the edge of the world. Everybody knew we were nowhere.

My American Metal (Blog Entry): *August 2*
The camp psychiatrist said there was no understanding people like Rainwater, that we can only understand ourselves. I told her I couldn't sleep, that I was having dreams of people without eyes. She said I should write about what

happened, and I told her I didn't know how to start. She said it's easier in steps, like a cooking recipe. I told her that was a fucked up thing to say, except I didn't say "fucked up." She said it helps to think about it differently to move past it.

My American Metal (Blog Entry): *August 3*

~~Total Time:~~ 30 minutes

~~4 Privates~~

~~1 Specialist~~

~~3 Corporals~~

~~2 Staff Sergeants~~

~~2 Second Lieutenants~~

~~1 Captain~~

~~1 Translator~~

~~Sand~~

~~1 Professional Size Volleyball~~

~~1 Volleyball Net~~

~~1. Set daytime temperature to 120 degrees. Place Privates, Sergeants, Lieutenants, and Captain in a 60' by 30' sand court. Play volleyball until sweating.~~

~~2. Simmer Specialist with pinch of psychosis, jealousy, or opiate. Set aside.~~

~~3. Add Translator. Simmer 25 minutes with non-stop New York City talk. Remove Translator. Set aside.~~

~~4. Add Specialist with loaded handgun. Whisk Specialist, Translator, and players in a large court. Keep whipping into frenzy for two minutes as others react with their firearms until the Specialist is no longer alive.~~

My American Metal (Blog Entry): *October 18*
We got the names and emails of our replacements. It wasn't soon enough.

My American Metal (Blog Entry): *December 25*
We spent our last night at the bar toasting cable television, indoor plumbing, and real hamburgers. A few soldiers mentioned the names of the ghosts we left. Somebody said, "Goddamn Rainwater," and everybody fell dead quiet.

I could almost stand by the end of the night. I think I asked Lee Marie to marry me. She said she thinks so if I quit trying to drown myself.

"There ain't enough water in the desert," I joked.

She said if anyone could drown himself in a glass of whiskey, it would be me.

My American Metal (Blog Entry): *June 5–backdated*
I remember it was 120 degrees. The sand whipped like flecks of red-hot metal off a grinding wheel. We had a few hours, so we raked a volleyball court. Dover played in high school. Captain Vega too. Nobody wanted Sabir, the interpreter, on their team. He was good at his translating. Had no idea when it came to sports. He paced the sidelines, smoking cigarettes, talking, talking, talking. Mostly about New York City. Just named things: Sarah Jessica Parker, Empire State Building, Bob Dylan.

"You know Bob Dylan?" Sabir asked.

I said, "Bob Dylan's a robot."

He laughed, and asked, "It's like Disney Land?"

"New York?" I said, but I'd never been. "Yeah. Exactly."

I remember this part real good because it was like he started dancing, spinning on his heels. But when he faced me, he wasn't grinning. It happened too fast. The gunshot, the blood. Shot in the neck. Still talking, talking, talking.

"Coney Island. Ellis Island," Sabir said. "Miley Cyrus."

He fell, and I fell with him. Grabbed his neck, pushing his wound hard, like I could snap his spinal cord. "Shut the fuck up!"

He said, "I love New York," until he couldn't speak.

Dover and Vega sprinted for the jeep. More gunshots. More yelling. It was Rainwater, pistol drawn, firing like a lunatic. But it didn't make any sense in my head.

Dover, ten feet from the jeep, dropped, a punch of blood on his chest. His head bobbed like he had fallen asleep, his legs giving.

I remember this about Specialist Rainwater:

- He was a middle child.
- Said he had a girlfriend in Knoxville.
- Was afraid of swimming in the ocean.
- Owned a hunting dog, Buck.
- He didn't hunt.
- He was on medication for anxiety.
- And he was also in love with Private Brian Dover.

And I remember never saying goodbye to him.

Other Animals

WIN WASN'T HOMELESS, which set him apart from the others. But he'd hit rock-bottom, jobless and sharing enough to be one among them. In the fifty-station clinic, they were strapped to centrifuge machines, fists clenching, unclenching, as their blood beat through clear lines, transforming into plasma in the bags suspended above. They wore paper-thin shirts and denim jeans and canvas jackets, and all carried an acrid stink, their faces skeletal and hollow-eyed. Some straight off of binges but ready to jump back on. And just like them, Win would collect his twenty-five-dollar payout and head downtown.

Nurses in lab coats roamed the floor as machines sucked and whirred, like animals feeding. First-timers were paid fifty, the clinic's hook. Regulars received half. The process lasted an hour, but it set you back three days, like being lost in a fog, as your body built nutrients back up again. One

smoke or beer after put you down hard, like a sledgeham-
mer to the head, but it was a good cheap buzz.

In a former life, Win taught algebra and consulted at
GE. People told him he looked like he should be on TV.
But none of that mattered when he had been asked the
same old questions in the lobby: Have you used this week?
Have you shared a needle? Have you had unprotected sex
with a man? Have you *whatever*, to which he answered no,
the only answer he could give for the money.

Win's phlebotomist was a seven-foot tall African, pin-
thin with kind, ovoid eyes like soft-boiled eggs. He had never seen the man before, but his nametag read, "Chinonso,"
and he smelled like cinnamon toast. Win hadn't eaten yet
and might spare a couple bucks to buy a fast food burger,
but he couldn't concentrate because Chinonso's gait was
unimaginably long. Win counted in his head, one, two,
two and a half, waiting for Chinonso's log-sized foot to hit
the floor again. He wanted to tell Chinonso that he could
own a Guinness Record, but his head felt like a cotton ball
and he said, "You move like a cat."

Chinonso sat Win in an empty station. It reminded
Win of an upright Army cot, the hard frame pressing into
him. Chinonso carefully tore a plastic bag and unwrapped
a clear tube, attaching it to the centrifuge machine. His
gestures were drawn-out and seamless, like the rest of him,
his arms moving like algebraic expressions.

"Never met anyone named that." Win pointed at the
nametag.

"It was my *brudda's* name," Chinonso said.

"Your *who*?" Win asked, because he liked the sound.

"My *brudda*."

Win had read that Johann was passed down three times in the Bernoulli family. He wondered if names worked like the brachistochrone problem. The rapid descent of a name sliding from one son to another under the influence of gravity.

"It sounds like a good name," Win said. "I got a twin brother, Bill. B-I-L-L."

Chinonso smiled with big square teeth.

"No *sistas*?" Chinonso asked. "*Sistas* are nice. Most beautiful. Like gold queens."

"No royal *sistas* here," Win said, looking around.

"No," Chinonso said. "Not here, just royal blood."

Chinonso wrapped a blood pressure cuff around Win's bicep, inflating the antecubital vein. He handed Win a rubber tube shaped like a BMX handgrip.

"It will help the blood be pumped." Chinonso positioned Win's hand and squeezed the rubber grip to demonstrate. "Do like this, yes."

Chinonso sterilized Win's forearm with iodine and inserted a thick needle. Blood shot into the shaft and the plastic line grew fat and purple, and the machine separated the plasma.

"Chinsy," Win said. "Fuel's getting low." If he played it right, he could double-up on snacks. "Maybe you got those protein bars in the back?"

"Rest easy," Chinonso said.

Televisions were mounted to the walls with the same

movie playing. Police cruisers chasing an Aston Martin through wet city streets. The Martin cornered hard, a ninety-degree turn, and a cruiser crashed and exploded, flames shooting two stories high.

The man in the chair beside Win yipped like a hyena. He was a regular and wore a full-faced ski mask, the visible skin marked by sores and scabs.

"Hey. Pal. Buddy." An urban camo jacket hung over his knees as he shook with cold. He said his name was Trapper John and that he was sensitive to low temperatures and had scoliosis and was allergic to oxygen, which made him rashy, hence the sores.

Win ignored him, but Trapper John called again. "President's putting cancer in your drinking water. And all the gays are robots."

At twenty-nine, Win thought he had lost it all: his job, his girl, his health—only to realize there was always more to give, like a mind.

"They freeze you on purpose," Trapper John said. "They say it's saline to keep the veins open, but I had it in my veins. Saline, gasoline, liquid dream, A-team. Guarantee it's clam juice. Say, you're not a regular, I mean a Gold Club Member." Trapper John bit his lip, blowing a fleck of skin. "Question. I've been here how many times? Answer. Two thousand five hundred and thirty-three hundred. Say, you wouldn't know where vampires keep their gold? A blood bank. Get it? We could be blood brothers."

Win counted to himself and clenched his fist—one, two, squeeze; one, two, squeeze. The machine separated red-blood cells and plasma before his stripped-out blood returned. His arm felt cool, but after a moment the machine began drawing again, and he warmed.

Across the room, Chinonso sipped from a coffee mug. The top of his bald head nearly touched the ceiling. Win waved, hungry, and Chinonso raised his hand chest high. The room filled with movie sounds, explosions and gunshots. Win tried yelling over the noise, but his voice felt like dust in his mouth.

"We could be partners," Trapper John said. "Are you listening? Hey! Can you reach my water? I got a million bullions in the real world. And I'd split it with you."

On the pushcart between them was a Dixie cup.

"Freakin' thirsty," Trapper John said. "They take the water from your blood. We're made of ninety-seven percent water like the earth. They want pure blood because it cures cancer. That's what plasma is. Jesus was made of water not blood. He turned blood into water and cured Mary Magdalene. His last miracle. Now the President wants it." Trapper John reached for the cup again.

Win eased into his chair, staring at the ceiling, counting the stains on the panels, one shaped like a finch's beak. He thought maybe bloodstains. He was thirsty too, but he wanted to fill his bag and leave.

"I need my water," Trapper John said. "That's my water. Please, sugarman."

Win's bag was two-thirds full. It looked like piss. He'd read that it went to hemophiliacs and burn victims—people who could die waiting—but it wasn't free. Sold for thousands of dollars, and he got a fraction. If he could separate the plasma on his own, he could sell it on Craigslist. Even as a joke, someone would buy it.

But for now, his plasma and Trapper John's and the rest was all mixed up and shipped in rigs around the country, trailer loads full of biohazard drums. They were the heroes and the saviors, not the cops and the firemen. He liked knowing that the dying banker on the street, the man who shunned him for eating out of a garbage can, would come begging for his help. He imagined the news headline: "Bum Saves America."

Trapper John groaned. Win considered the Dixie cup. If he moved his elbow wrong, the needle would gouge deep. But he swung his arm, a wide, slow pivot. Robotic. But short of the cup. Trapper John shook his head and stepped from his chair, his foot landing with a thud, and he reached. He silenced the room, letting out a wail as the needle drove into his forearm. His scream hung in the air like a phantom. Nurses rushed, and Win counted. One, two, three, four, five, six. They lifted Trapper John, his arms outstretched like Christ on the cross. His lips moved, and Win thought he might be saying "Bingo" over and over.

"Chinsy," Win said, as Chinonso passed. "You bring my protein bars?"

Chinonso looked at Win as if he was something evil among them. Win fidgeted because everything was happening too quickly. His plasma bag was full, but it could be another twenty minutes by the time they got to him. More nurses circled Trapper John, and under his mask Win saw he was grinning.

Win felt sorry for him, and the nurses, and all the others in the clinic because this was as good as it got. But Win wouldn't gouge himself for the attention. He had sworn that he'd never let his life slip that far gone. And if it did, he imagined he could get back to something like the beginning.

Win flinched as he slid the needle from his arm, releasing a small squirt of blood. He pressed the wound with two fingers, and stole the bag of plasma from the hook, tucking it under his shirt. He passed through the waiting room without a word and out the front doors.

His brother Bill stood on the sidewalk and offered Win a smoke.

"You get paid?" Bill asked, sucking feverishly on his cigarette. "I bet you did. Tell me, am I right?"

From beneath his shirt, Win showed him the bag, and the plasma shined like gold.

"What the hell is that?" Bill asked.

"As good as it gets," Win said.

It was only a matter of time before they would log in to a computer at the library and open a Craigslist account. They would title the listing: *Real Plasma - Cures Cancer – Like New.* They would ask for $200, enough for fast food all week and some left over, maybe for crank. "One last time," Win would say, "to celebrate second chances."

Last Days at Wolfjaw

Do NOT GO outside. Glimpses of marsh look pleasant. The water is clean like metal. Ripe foliage two-feet-long, fleshy. But swaths of black flies and doughy maggots cover everything. The terrible smell cuts your throat.

Fisk, across river, pierced by a proboscis as long as a sword. Straight into his gut on his hammock. A ten-foot bug, according to the story. Conroy, Davilyn's father, saw it in his binoculars. Fisk's eyes popped open, possessed. In a second, the bug shot into the air, Fisk rising two hundred feet, mouth wide without words.

But Grandpa Conroy is dead, and I've never seen a bug thicker than my fist. There were millions though. Davilyn says, "People survive worse." Nukes. The Holocaust. Even the dinosaurs. "We'll get through it," she says.

She thinks our little girl is out there. Four years gone would make Auburn six. "Didn't have her long enough to

find her way home." I never said this to Davilyn. Grandpa Conroy had reminded his daughter daily that he could
feel her out there. "Flies had her." But I wouldn't say this
either.

We screened the porch before the cough hit. And before the flies. Now they blackout every window. The cough
is how it began with Conroy, and Davilyn. She won't eat
today. Once you stop, you don't start. Stopped drinking
too. We have another day. "Two," I say aloud. I stare at the
porch wood. Gray and split and old. Soon the house will
collapse right under us.

Years back, the buzzing seemed to stop altogether. The
relentless fly-hum as constant as silence, and then I could
not tell sound from no sound. But I hear Auburn's cough.
Wispy. Brown. Children were the first.

We had entirely different lives. I taught at the college.
Davilyn too. She was in workshop when it happened. News
said we had thirty minutes from first cough to contagion.
I ran her into the woods, behind the house, deep into the
swamp. If she was breathing, I couldn't submerge her. I
tied her in my jacket. She was a beautiful monster wedged
in the branches of the muskeg spruce. Auby was a good
girl. Auby never cried. I heard her cough, and a distant
chainsaw rumbling, and "Daa, daaa." Those dark sounds
as I dragged away.

Davilyn is finally sleeping, but the coughing only stops
once. Asleep, I tell myself. The silence is undeniable, and
I push against the porch door. Hinges stuck with rust. Finally cracking loose. Swings open. Hungry. Thousands of

flies cling to the screen, the walls outside, and the trees. Blackest black waiting. I clap my hands. "C'mon," I say. Each eye with four thousand lenses. I see them see millions of me. "It's for you, tenders."

The Path of Lightning

PICTURE PUNCHING AND kicking some dude in the head. The MMA cage. A thousand shrieking spectators. Then an arm cinches around your neck. The squeeze of a python. Breathing through a straw until the straw is gone, and the air is gone. The moment before you crash out, you get this high. Without air, you see Buddha sitting cross-legged on the greenest grass, sipping a warm cup of golden milk, grinning like everything means everything. That's part of the reason I fought for so long. Winning was euphoric, but losing was euphoric too.

The weeks leading up to that last fight, my gigantic face was on a billboard on Las Vegas Boulevard. Oskar "Thunder Struck" Jones versus Johnny "Little Nevada" Ramirez.

"Little Nevada" was born in Carson City, but his parents moved to California when he was six months old. Still, the nickname earned him an extra grand whenever he fought in Vegas, and mine was "Thunder" after three straight wins by knockout.

The fight against Little Nevada looked like this. He came out punch-hungry. Tried to land an atomic bomb, but I kicked his ankle. As he toppled, I bopped him on his ears like I was crashing two cymbals.

I liked Little Nevada as a person, but in the ring, I blasted him in the forehead with a knee. It was a missile, and I felt his skull break the way you feel a pint glass crack when you hit it against a wall. A flap of skin around his eye dangled like a dog's tongue.

Little Nevada dropped to his knees, wobbling; I waited for the ref and the ref shrugged. Through my mouthguard, I said, "Call it."

Little Nevada said something, like "Fight me," but gurgled.

The ref said, "Keep fighting."

"Look at him," I said, but the fans weren't having it. Some booed; others yelled, "Finish him!"

I was about to murder my friend in front of all those people, but I never saw it coming—he found life. He swiped me with a leg, and down I went. Hit the mat hard, and he pulled my arm under my chin. Bicep pinched against my throat. All the air stopped. Everything got heavy. Lights in the ring going white, then red, then dark. Then I saw a smiling beautiful Buddha sipping a warm cup of milk. But everything meant nothing to me.

Instead of tapping out, I flailed. Tried to thump him anywhere—his Adam's apple, his dick—to break his grip.

But the world disappeared, and when I woke up, Little Nevada was surrounded by the med staff and ringside doctor. The ref tried to lift his arm in victory, but the ringside doc yelled at him to take it easy. The crowd booed ten minutes straight.

It's funny how you can train day and night for one thing—battle. And when you don't know anything else, that part of the brain doesn't know how to shut itself off. I don't think he was even conscious when he choked me out; he was a dead robot.

$9,000 to lose a fight. But I was done *almost* killing people in the ring. I needed a normal life. But that would start in the morning.

For the rest of the night, I was still the fighter on the billboard on Las Vegas Boulevard, and I was staying my last night at the Venetian on the thirty-third floor. There were two of them waiting at my room when I got there. Tiffany or Tina or Trish and the other one. I'll never forget his name—Charlie, with the bright red lipstick. Trish had the keycard in the door, and Charlie pushed it open. I caught my reflection in the hallway mirror, and my face looked like a smashed plum. I never heard the door close because they both let their clothes fall to the floor, and all I could see were fake tits and giant pecks. Trish grabbed my hand and guided my index finger into her mouth, while Charlie with the red, red lips tugged down my jeans and found the head of my half-erect cock like it was a red, red magnet. As if they had practiced together a hundred times, every time Trish glided her mouth around my knuckle, so did Charlie.

When I looked down, his red lips were kissing my pubic hair, but when he drew back, it was the unpainted inner lip—pale and pink—that pulled out by the contact along my flesh that amazed me. Of the fake tits and giant pecks and red lips and their matching bleached blonde hair, the pale, pink strip of lip seemed like the most real thing I saw in the room. But a fighter is paid to fight, and they were paid to fuck. It was my last night before this all went away.

Sexy Super Mario, sexy police officer, sexy Little Red Riding Hood, and sexy Statue of Liberty. But I wore boxing gloves and a white bathrobe to Pat and Sam's Halloween party. We met in Psychology class at community college.

I waited in line for beer. Four guys in black ski masks doing keg stands. The woman dressed as a priest in front of me called them girls. She wore her hair under a bald cap.

"Let's go already," she said.

When they finished, the tap line only puffed foam into her cup.

"Mind if I help, *padre?*" I said, pumping the keg.

"As long as you confess your sins, champ."

I filled her cup. Then mine.

"We'd both be here a while."

"Then I'll take a raincheck," she said, grinning.

In a bedroom, Pat spun dubstep. Strobe light blinking black then light. A merry gang of red-masked ghouls and sexy, bare-skinned kittens. There, gone, there again. Jumping, flailing. Pat wore a brown three-piece suit with a two-foot-high green wig. A stop-motion tree from another world. I missed the clown racing across the room. Rico-

THE PATH OF LIGHTNING

cheting off a ghoul, a kitten, and then me, knocking the red cup from my hand. I could see the liquid leap the crest of the cup, disappearing with the blackout, but light again, and sloshing onto the floor.

I was a fighter, so I fought. The familiar instinct to block and jab. I cocked my arm and bombed the clown in the jaw. In that stop-motion scene, the clown's curly red hair flew off, neck rocked back, feet lifting off the floor. A sound of a body smacking down hard enough to stop the music.

The red wig and fake nose had fallen off. It was Sam.

"The boxer hit her," someone said.

Everyone in the house shoved me outside. The sky was a black gown of judgment, and distant sirens echoed. The police were out there somewhere. They weren't out for me, but they should've been. The guys in ski masks said they were going to hunt me down.

To my back, I heard, "Hey, tough guy. I'm talking to you."

I said, "Walk away."

"I thought you could confess your sins now," the priest from the party said. Without her wig, her black hair hung past her shoulders. "Aren't you well-mannered? You always go around hitting trans girls?"

"Don't fuck with me."

"But I want to fuck with you."

"Seriously," I said. "Not tonight."

"If you get bored later," she said, "Google me. 'Harley Camming.' Like the motorcycle."

WE met at See See Motorcycles & Coffee Shop. At the table in the corner, I saw the camgirl from the Internet videos. Harley smiled, but I looked away—maybe this wasn't my best idea.

She stood up to hug me. "I'm surprised you showed up."

"Maybe I'm just a royal pervert."

"Perversion is in the eyes of the beholder."

We talked until my coffee went cold. She told me she wanted to be a horse vet when she was a little girl. I told her I wanted to be a boxer since I can remember. All morning, bikers came and went. Tattoos, leather, and piercings. But it was all on the surface. Were they really that tough, careless, and wild? Maybe that's what they saw when they looked at me and Harley. Or maybe they saw a sex worker and a broke-ass boxer.

I said, "Is camming the worst thing you ever did?"

"Is this a test?"

"Are you good at tests?" I asked.

Harley said, "According to my mother, yes. According to the men who pay me, no. What about you? What's the worst thing you've ever done?"

"I nearly killed a man," I said. "But I was paid to. Still, he was my friend."

"We're both a little broken," she said, reaching past my cold coffee to tug on my knuckle. "Maybe that gives us a chance to fix things, right?"

Her grip was enough. When she blinked, I looked at her black-pearl eyes, opening to take me into her mind, her body.

HARLEY woke at 6:30 a.m. Kissed my cheek twice before she slid out of bed and set her laptop on the floor to watch a yoga workout on YouTube. I pretended I was asleep for a few minutes, then drifted off for another hour.

I woke to the sound of a blender, and I put on her pink terry bathrobe. She stood at the kitchen counter and poured her smoothie into a mason jar. A schedule on the fridge held by a magnet, a red tomato.

1. Wake up @ 6:30 a.m. for yoga
2. Breakfast: Drink green tea / Eat toast with avocado & garlic salt / Smoothie
3. Jog 30 minutes OR work out 60 minutes
4. Sheet mask & shower
5. Lunch: Smoothie (one banana, blueberries, greens), quinoa salad
6. Make-up time / take publicity photos / update & respond to social media
7. Clean room / wash toys & prep computer, camera equipment
8. Dinner: Rice pasta with protein (tofu, soy curls, or black beans)
9. Live feed for 4-6 hours
10. 11 p.m. - 12:00 a.m. Shower / bed

Then she noticed me. "You're good-looking, even in that thing."

"Come here," I said.

"I don't take orders."

"But what if I want you for breakfast," I said.

"Then kneel down and eat me."

I took a knee, and I looked up at her like I was about to propose, but her hand was already on my head, pulling my face into her crotch. Through her yoga pants, I could smell her—ripe and loamy—and my cock stiffened.

"I know we just met," she said, "and I'm not trying to push you away or pull you into something, but I'm not some slut."

I said, "Why would I think that?"

"Because I'm going to ask you if I can film you right now."

I stared up at her. "What do you want me to say?"

"I could give you half of whatever people pay," she said.

"You think I want to fuck you for some loser's money?"

EVEN after that, it wasn't long before we moved in together. A brick apartment building on Hawthorne Avenue two blocks from the old Hawthorne Strip. For a time, Portland was dirty. Real dirty. Every other business was a dive bar or a strip joint. Now it was an idealistic dream made for an Apple commercial. But the problem with a utopia is the original Greek means *no place*. I remember someone saying that in my Creative Writing class.

I met with the writing instructor after class about his recommendations on how to become a serious writer. He said unless my mom was a real cunt, then I should resort to hitchhiking to Alaska and working at a fishery for the life experience. He said the writer Vonnegut had both—a crazy family and a wild life.

At home, I threw my backpack on the floor. Tracked dirt and dried leaves across the kitchen. Harley had wrapped a plate of food in tin foil and left it on the stove.

I listened at the bathroom door, the shower running.

"It's me," I said, letting myself in.

The spray from the detachable showerhead against her pussy looked impressive in the live feed—her laptop on the sink capturing the entire scene.

"I'm camming," she said.

"Thanks for the food," I said. "That's all."

Before I shut the door, I heard her say, "That is my boyfriend, Big Derek, and it would take a lot more than two hundred tokens to convince him to fuck me."

The Internet had a way of remembering faces, and I didn't want to jeopardize any real work I might have lined up after my degree.

I lied to get the interview. The job entailed monitoring developmentally challenged pedophiles who had been adjudicated by the courts. It paid $14 an hour, but I needed a clean driving record and no criminal past. The latter always screwed things up.

A high wooden fence surrounded the complex. At the front gate, I pressed a silent buzzer.

"You must be Oskar," a woman wearing only teal said as she opened the gate. "I'm Miss Sharon, the manager of Comfort House."

In the courtyard, four guys played basketball; they all waved.

One, who was noticeably shorter than the others and grinned too wide like he didn't know what he was happy about, greeted me.

"Wow, you're tall. I'm Dennis," he said. "Is he like us, Miss S?"

"Not like you. He's here to see if he wants to work with you."

"Please work here," Dennis said. "Everyone's a trouble-maker, but I'm not; and you're tall. I like tall men."

"I'll see what I can do, little man," I said.

"Okay, big man. I called him big man, Miss S. You hear that? We're friends."

In her office, Miss Sharon explained the details of the job. All the counselors were the same. None were junior or senior, but there was a staff lead each night. The staff lead was chosen at random by rolling dice at the start of the shift. Miss Sharon told me that counselors monitored the residents for inappropriate behavior and to prevent them from handling inappropriate material, as well as ensuring the house rules, including hygiene, were always met.

"Anything to do with children is inappropriate," Miss Sharon said. "You can't have pictures of children, and if a commercial with children in it comes on during TV time, clients need to look away, or else they get punished."

"And punishment means what exactly?"

"The usual," she said. "We might take away one of their privileges. Dennis, for instance, we confiscate his PlaySta-tion. If that doesn't work, then a homework assignment. That's up to you though."

"And they're all pedophiles?"

"I'm sure you read the job description carefully."

"I did," I said.

"Shifts are straightforward," Miss Sharon continued. "You cook dinner with your client. You make sure they clean up and shower, and if they can't follow the rules..."

"I take away the PlayStation."

"You're a fast learner. But there is one thing I wanted to talk about. On your application, you wrote that you had no criminal record."

"I did write that," I said.

"That's what I thought." Her tone changed. "Each applicant gets put into a database, so we always run a background check for red flags. And, well, I'm not sure we can offer you the position."

My heart pounded. "Then what am I doing here?"

"I was hoping you might be able to explain," she said. "You see, our clients have histories of violence too. And maybe you can teach them how to manage it. I don't mean to pry, but assault is a sobering red flag."

Maybe I could make a difference in these men's lives; Miss Sharon thought so. No one else had given me a chance to interview.

"I nearly beat a man to death," I said, bluntly. "I was young. It was a bar fight. If I could go back, I'd change everything. But I can't. I can learn from it, though, right?"

"And what did you learn from it?"

I should've paused, but I said honestly, "After you do it once, it gets easier."

I drove home passing derelict men and women huddled under bridges and camped out in tents on sidewalks. I figured it could never be me, but I could count three things that needed to happen for me to end up alongside them. Not getting a job, hitting the bottle too hard, and beating a stranger in a random parking lot to a pulp.

HARLEY played Jenga on the kitchen floor. Her viewers paid her to pull blocks. When the tower fell, she let them decide how she would come. Sometimes her fingers, sometimes anal beads. But she wouldn't squirt unless they bought a private show.

It was never real, though, because she showed me the dildo she filled with water. A thousand strangers from around the world watched, and she knew a dozen of them would tip twenty bucks for her squirt show. Pumping her dildo, her slow moan would quicken and grow, and with each chime of the electronic tips, her moan would rise above them. Three hundred dollars later, she set the show to private, pumped the dildo like she was about to come and when she released the water switch, it would spray all over like a geyser.

By the time her live feed ended, I was already in bed. She crawled next to me and breathed into my armpit. "You smell great. You should bottle it."

"Easy for you to say. No one's paying me for nothing."

"Cam with me," Harley said.

"Fuck that."

"Seriously. It's just money, and you need it. It can be that simple, can't it?"

For years, I knocked people out for money. And before that, I would do it for free. In the bars. On the streets. In dark back alleys. I lured people into fighting just to smash their teeth in.

Maybe I felt like sparring with her. I said, "I want to do something I can feel good about. Something noble."

"Noble? Who the fuck are you, Sir Elton-fucking-John? That's a low blow, man. You should know better."

In a professional fight, I learned that letting a punch slip through, at least in the beginning, calms the nerves. You focus better.

"Then set it up," I said.

"Set what up?"

"Lights, camera, action. Fuck it. The way you see it, no one probably expects anything good to come of me, so why not let the world see the loser fighter be a loser cam boy."

When you're good, you see punches before they're even thrown. You can tell by your opponent's eyes or how they have their body angled. Maybe by the sudden tension in their cheek.

I stared her in the eyes, like black pearls, looking at my reflection. I could've been ten years old or a thousand, but then all I saw was her single tear that formed. The sadness was ageless and lived across all time. A simple bead of moisture, and behind it there were a thousand memories destroying her. A lifetime of stories. People telling her things like she's beautiful, she's got so much potential, and I'm sorry your father died, and it will get easier after your schooling, and it will get easier in a new city, and I always thought you'd do more with your life, and why would you do that, were you just acting out or are you that sick, and darling, sweet, sweet, darling, you were once so beautiful, and, again, you had so much potential, and now I have to walk away because you're no longer the child I bore.

It was everything I was ever told, too. Mostly.

I think I said, "I didn't mean it. You understand? Because I'm just like you, and together we can do things better. For us. Like you said, we're each a little broken, so we can fix each other. Together."

But maybe all I said was, "This isn't working anymore."

There was a fine line between that path to a clear victory and setting yourself up to get knocked out because maybe that one punch you let slip through earlier caught you just right. It was the thunder in the distance that lets you know lightning wasn't far off. But now you're not thinking clearly. Because really, what you thought was a language of strategy, telling you what to do next, was only the steady red-beat of a warning bell summoning you closer and closer and closer to the end.

Descendants of the Crow

THE GIRL IN the blue bikini hurled herself from the ledge of Crow Creek Falls. She was number six. The only remaining evidence was the white ribbon in her hair, now wrapped around a reedy branch protruding the river's glassy surface. All girls, but no bodies found. The mystery I was called to.

Then Jessalynn—fifteen years old, freckled with strawberry blonde hair—seconds later, sprinted toward the edge. She was number seven

THE Crow Creek Falls theories began with the pressure kids faced in school: ACT and SAT scores, potential scholarships, and how many social media followers they had, as if the absence of a viral video on their YouTube channel by the age of fifteen justified vaulting themselves to their doom.

The move from Chapmanokoma County happened a month earlier, and I was assigned to the Crow Creek

Falls cases. My brother, Gary, still lived in Chapmanoko-ma Hamlet. Gary was a good guy, three years older; but he ate too much, and he drank too much. His cholesterol bumped 215, and if he stroked out—but lived—someone would have to take care of him until his dying day. I told myself he'd be okay. It was enough to make the seven-hour drive apart seem okeydokey.

Gary texted me a picture of his swollen leg—ankle the color of a baked ham hock, skin bloated like it was about to tear apart.

Does this look infected?

It was common for Gary to text me about his health: the obvious gout, or some drunk-related self-inflicted infection, food poisoning from two-day-old unrefrigerated chicken wings, or the almost-always sky-rocketing blood pressure results.

You need to go to the ER, I wrote, but I knew he wanted me to write, *No. It looks fine.*

If I responded with anything other than a joke, he went silent.

You're going to die if you don't do something, I wrote. *You there?*

Then I wrote, *Are you ignoring me?*

Then I stopped texting too.

JESSALYNN was the most recent one who vanished.

I started my interviews with Crane, her boyfriend. Said he saw the whole thing. Crane was sixteen years old: blonde hair and alarming zits. I sat across their kitchen table, yellow doilies under the mugs of weak black tea his mother, Doris, made.

My phone vibrated in my jean's pocket. "Excuse me," I said, but I didn't recognize the number. "What was that now?"

Crane said, "She was standing right there, but she was somewhere else, if that makes sense." He scratched a yellow-headed zit, and he tore the skin. "Then she was just gone."

"You mean she jumped?" I asked, and I handed him a napkin.

"No," he said, voice giving out, and he dabbed his zit with the napkin, releasing it when tears tripped across his rutted skin, and he wiped his face with his hand. "She looked destroyed. Like she was on another planet. That's when she jumped."

I offered him the same napkin again. "You saw her jump, but what do you think happened to her body?"

Crane squeezed the napkin in his fist. "It's a vortex like mirrors and sandpits," he said. "The river goes somewhere else. You don't know that?"

I sipped the weak black tea Doris had made as she watched us from the kitchen doorway.

Doris said, "The man's here to get answers, not to hear about those other dimensions."

"It's okay," I said, and stood to excuse myself. "We're all looking for answers. These things aren't easy."

Every interview amounted to the same thing. They began with a group of teens going to the bluffs to party, soak up the sun, drink, and make out. Until someone stopped talking, their eyes drifting off, looking defeated, and then dashing off the cliff.

Only Crane talked about some other dimension. Everyone else was certain the body had been swept beneath by the handsy undertow from the water letting out a mile upstream at the Conklingville Dam.

THE next weekend, I drove back to Chapmanokoma Hamlet. Parked outside Gary's yellow house. I could see him on the couch through the window from the road. Maybe he was watching TV. All the lights on inside. His arms moving like molasses, slowly forcing sip after sip of vodka down his throat.

I texted, *How you feeling tonight, bud?*

He looked down at his phone.

I texted, *I'm just concerned, but I'll stop bothering you.*

He seemed upset, concentrating maybe.

A text flashed on my phone. *In another world, I'm a vegan and I run marathons. Don't worry about me. Believe me.*

He must've drank an entire liter of vodka before I started the trip home. Before I left, I wrote, *I'd like to meet him— Gary the Vegan.*

NUMBER seven's mother preferred to be called Ms. Ambrose. She had Jessalynn's laptop password. Showed me her full Google history.

That was how I found the online forum.

Ms. Ambrose said, "Jessie always talked about the Descendants."

She paced in her living room, and I sat on the couch; but every time Ms. Ambrose started in a new direction, I began to stand, thinking we were going to another part of the house, but she'd reverse her course every time.

She told me, "They weren't a cult or a religious group, but strangers who had stories to tell about crows. Phobias, run-ins in the wild, stories of them attacking dogs or this one time a child at the playground."

"The crows?"

"They said it was all about the ancient Greeks who thought the crow was Apollo—a sort of prophecy. You can read their comments. It's all the same thing."

"And this is what Jessalynn talked to her friends about?"

"They were obsessed," Ms. Ambrose said.

It was beginning to come together. Crow Creek Falls, the Descendants of the Crow, the jumpers looking into the sky before leaping—as if speaking to some visible, godlike crow. But the wacky theory of a phantom crow was not enough to bring to my boss.

I wasn't a tech addict, but I was addicted to the information. Needing to know when I needed to know was a problem. The Internet on my phone meant knowing the batting average of Willie Mays, or the number of time zones in the world, or at what temperature bacteria is killed, or when Gary gets my messages and why he doesn't respond. It meant instant knowledge, instant reassurance. It meant I knew everything. That was godlike

I watched Gary for decades drink himself to death, and

I'd been ready to get some final call from a stranger. "Your brother," the stranger would say. "I'm sorry."

I texted Gary, *Just curious. What dimension would you be vegan?*

He responded, *Pluto.*

That's a planet.

Then I'm vegan on another planet.

I wrote, *Why can't you be that here?*

But he was silent.

I asked Siri when my brother would die, and Siri said, "I don't see *brother* in your contacts. What is your brother's name?"

They say our dead are never dead until they are forgotten. But can you be alive if no one knows your name? Maybe Gary was already dead to the rest of the world.

THE bluffs at Crow Creek Falls peaked two hundred feet above the river. The parking lot crowded with cars a decade old. Stickers of high school mascots, punk bands, and silhouettes of pornographic Disney cartoons.

The lawn on the bluffs was a patchwork of blankets and thin, bronze bodies. I didn't feel my age, but if I closed my eyes, I could be one of them. Still, they did not see me—the old, invisible man. Every one of them with a smart phone. Texting and scrolling.

I stepped over a girl with a beer can in one hand and her phone in the other. Unphased. Drawn into the world in her palm.

"Pardon," I said, to a boy in the same state. He didn't answer.

I clapped and shouted, "Hey."

Fingers curled around my pistol grip. I imagined that I could take aim, but they wouldn't see me. Would they? Too suppressed by information. Where infinity does not mean everything but nothing. They were buried in nothingness.

I said, "Do you know about the jumpers?"

A girl in yellow cat-eye frames, maybe Jessalynn's age, looked up. Did she see me? In her reflective lenses, I was there in a white collared shirt. This was my face. See me?

But she raised her phone to the sky and took a selfie.

It seemed like they were gone, ghosts into another world. The Internet was the fifth dimension. No past, no present. I looked at the sky. Crows flying in a circle, a ring of black knots. But crows don't fly in circles.

I texted Gary, *You'll never believe what I'm seeing.*

We were inseparable as kids. I'd crawl into his bed; he'd tell me he'd take me with him everywhere. To different states, different countries. We'd fly all over the world. But he was in Chapmanokoma, and I was here.

Reflected in the water, the crows made a circle like a portal. Maybe to where Gary was vegan. Maybe to where the girls were alive. Maybe I could go there too.

Held in Place by Teeth
that Face Inward

THE SMELL INSIDE the old house slid under my skin. One breath. Burrowing under my ribs—far, far into the center. That was where the hole had always been.

Stepping into Grandma Dee's kitchen was a time machine. Zapped back. The yellow wallpaper, the edge of the counter where I cracked my head, and the AM/FM radio playing call-in talk shows, people groaning about the new Walmart or garbage day changing from Tuesday to Thursday. Ten thousand memories of childhood.

Now—spaghetti dinner with sausage. Grandma Dee's go-to.

I had quit drinking, so I could save enough for a plane ticket home. Driving for Lyft wasn't turning me into the millionaires I envied on MTV *Cribs*.

Gram wouldn't shut up about Russell. Like a dying

wish, she said, "I can bake a ham. Boil carrots with honey. He's your brother. You should eat together."

I couldn't tell her to put a plug in it, so I forked half my plate of spaghetti—twirling until there was too much.

"Your mother was stubborn," she said.

"You don't need to bring her up."

"Your father too."

The last time I saw Russell we had talked about a school shooting. We were probably slamming Mich Lights at some bar, and I said something like, "Fuck automatic weapons," and Russ said, "Are we going to ban kitchen knives after somebody gets stabbed?" and I said, "Kids are dead, asshole," and he said, "A kiddie rapist isn't going to not rape kiddies because there's a law. It's in their DNA." Then I probably left him at that bar because driving drunk was the better option.

But Grandma Dee never gave up on us. With my mouth full of spaghetti, she held up a sheet of loose-leaf paper from the counter.

"I wrote his address down. Ask him if he wants a ham dinner, or I can make *pierogies*."

Maybe this really was her dying wish.

TECHNICALLY, Russell lived on waterfront property because his singlewide was parked next to a pond. He raised a handful of pigs and worked at the Walmart distribution center. Television light flashed through his curtains, and I cupped my hands to a window, but I couldn't see inside. The television went black, and the door opened. Russell trained the .22 on me, firing over my shoulder.

"Freeze, dickhead."

I stepped into a spider web, raised my arms.

"I got *pierogies*."

Webbing stuck to my lips. When we were little, a barn spider lived in Russell's windowsill at Grandma Dee's. He'd point out every single mummified fly, and say, "Some people are spiders, but we got fly genes."

Russell reached inside and flipped a switch. The porch light glowed.

"Cabbage or cheese?" Russ asked, about the *pierogies*.

"Are you nuts?"

"If I knew it was you, I wouldn't have missed," he said, simpering.

"Told Gram I'd make sure you're still alive, and you are, so I'll get going."

It seemed like a full minute passed before he said, "You want a beer?"

"I ain't drinking, but I'll watch you."

He brought out two cans of Milwaukee's Best. Handed me one, but I didn't crack the tab. We talked about the weather; it felt safe. I told him it rained six months out the year in Oregon. He said he couldn't stand the Adirondack winters anymore.

The night was dead still until a car pulled into his driveway. You could hear the gravel under the tires from a football field away. Then the pulse of a red strobe light. Reminded me of freshman year in high school with Brandon Delaney; his pink-haired girlfriend, Tiffany; and her brother, Cam, who played drums in *DAIN BRAMAGE*. Leaving the school grounds, we smoked cigarettes and dreamed about all the big venues we were going to play when we got famous. A pickup of rednecks from our grade—Kyle Manning, Chip Bartone, and the nose-guard on the varsity team, Ronny Jablonski—drove past. Called us fags, and we flipped them off, too stupid to be scared. The truck braked hard, and Chip jumped out. He whipped a PowerLock tape measure like a split-seam fastball, and Brandon Delaney dropped. The tape measure bounced off the side of his head like it was made of rubber. Brandon writhed on the ground, and after a long growl from the pickup's engine as they took off, a puddle of crimson blood poured out of Brandon's ear.

Tiffany screamed, "Motherfuckingcocksuckers," and Cam grabbed a handful of gravel, but none of their efforts were going to stop the bleeding.

I raced back to Russell's locker. Told him the breathless truth. When we got back, one of the teachers was loading Brandon into her car. Trooper Nowack, who was also the assistant JV football coach, was already at the school and talking to Tiffany and Cam.

"Tiff says you know the boys who did this," Trooper Nowack said.

Russell said, "My brother just come and get me, but he told me they were kids from Fonda. Taunting us and what-not."

"Is that true?" Trooper Nowack asked.

I nodded, and Russell said, "See?"

We watched Brandon get driven off, and Trooper Nowack followed them to the hospital.

"Why didn't you tell him?" I asked.

Russell said, "If they got a chance to do that to us, we get a chance to do that to them. You understand? If we damn told on them, we wouldn't get that chance. It's only fair."

Even before Mom left Dad and Dad took off, we were trouble as kids; the whole town was trouble. A week after Brandon Delaney bled what seemed like half of his brain out of his ear, me and Russell lugged a backpack full of bricks to Kyle Manning's house. That was justice. In the middle of the night, we threw every single one of them through the windshield of his pickup. But for Russell, justice meant taking it even further. He reached into another bag, and he filled an empty beer bottle with lighter fluid and stuffed a rag deep into the neck.

"You want to light it?" he whispered in the dark.

We weren't there to burn a house down, were we?

I said, "This is stupid."

"Fuck it," he said, and when the bottle smashed against the house, a flash of yellow fire belched from the shadows. A whoosh of chaos, like all the evil in the world was made visible in one hot, fiery breath. The fire burned itself out within seconds, and the world returned to black, but even though no one could see us, we were there. No longer boys, but animals reborn. Fierce, blood-pumping, and criminal.

As if he could read my mind, Russ said, "Evil doesn't act out of a sense of justice."

"We gotta run," I said.

"Then they won't know not to fuck with us," he said.

"What are you talking about?"

"You go," Russ said. "I gotta stay so everybody in this shithole town knows not to fuck with us.

Arrested for the first time in his life, he was proud to own it.

TONIGHT, Trooper Nowack parked beneath Russell's tarpaulin carport. He opened his door, stepping tiredly on the gravel, and he limped around the nose of the cruiser.

"Haven't seen you in a few," Trooper Nowack said. "I was on my nightly, and the neighbors called about gunshots. Thought maybe night hunting, which you both know is illegal. You boys poaching?"

"New surround sound speakers," Russell said. "TV's getting real violent these days."

Trooper Nowack said, "Maybe so, but then I see something strange on your porch here, and legally speaking, you're not allowed to have firearms on the property, Russell. Not after last time. 'Cause that'd be pretty serious."

I watched Russell slide his hand down the railing toward the barrel of his .22.

"You're going to bust me for having a pea shooter?"

"I did drive all the way out here, so how about we fill out some paperwork at the station?" Trooper Nowack said. "That way your neighbors can get some sleep tonight."

I said it before I thought it. "It's mine. The gun."

"You look a lot like Russell's younger brother," Trooper Nowack said. "But he always had a good head on his shoulders."

"Don't be stupid," Russell said to me. "Nowack ain't as dumb as he looks. You mind following us?"

THE waiting room at the station was the same as it was fifteen years ago. Russ was a juvenile with a clean record back then. In and out. At least that's how I remembered it. We never really talked about it either, and we stopped being friends with Brandon Delaney too. Truth was, when he got out of the hospital, he was slower, like he had a different brain altogether. Nothing much happened to Chip Bartone, Kyle Manning, or Fat Ronnie. I even think Kyle got a new truck out of it.

The odds were stacked against some of us; we learned that young. But my brother was a hero. No one else was helping us.

The waiting room clock ticked off two hours before a guard told me Russell was being processed for release. His nametag read Stouffer, like the TV-dinner company.

"Just down the sidewalk," Stouffer said. "Second door to the left. You'll see a gray counter. There's no third door, so if you don't see nothing, you've gone too far."

"Nothing begets nothing," I said, the words just popping into my head.

RUSSELL buckled his seat belt, and all he said was, "Need a cold one."

The Snowed Inn was closest and was still open. Cheap beers, neon signs, plywood walls, and a jukebox. The only food on the menu was American cheese and white bread sandwiches. An hour or two until closing time.

"Been three months already?" the bartender said, when he saw Russell. He had a big bald head like a basketball.

"Happy to see me?" Russ said.

"You drink too much, and I'm going to crack your head open again."

Dylan Kaspersky. A.K.A. Bighead. He was the older brother of one of my classmates. Last I heard, he worked weekend gigs with a few bad *hombres* from Gloversville. The Gary Brothers. They owned a junk yard and sold anything they could get their hands on: bad speed, guns, computer data, you name it.

"That sounds fair," Russ said. "Now two Mich Lights and two shots of Fireball, please and thank you, *garçon*."

"Sprite," I said. "Slice of lime if you got it."

"A fucking slice of lime," Russ repeated, and hooted.

He made quick haste of both shots of Fireball, and I sipped my Sprite, scanning the ceiling. Dollars bills pinned like trophies. Behind the register was a photograph from the "great blizzard" when I was twenty-one. Everyone I knew who had transportation headed out for some adventure, but we always ended up in the same place.

When I left Perth way back, I left a lot of things. A girl named Kimmy Rose, who smoked too much pot and had two nipple rings, who had also been pregnant for a few weeks before she wasn't anymore, a brother who treated our relationship like a cactus—by ignoring it, and a grandmother who raised me like I was her own son.

I had no regrets back then. But now that I was back, and the only thing anyone ever asked of me was that I see Russ... well, here I was.

"Why keep pretending we like each other?" I blurted.

Russ held up a finger as he drank his beer. His Adam's

apple bobbed, and half the beer in his bottle was gone, and then all of it was gone.

"Oh, brother bear," he said. "You getting all emotional on me?"

I never intended to leave forever. I always wanted to buy some land, raise a kid with Kimmy; maybe Grandma Dee would spend her twilight years with us. But then bad shit happened, and I drove west; and the further I drove, the easier it was to never look back.

I said, "Gram begs me to see you, but if she only knew. You're the poster child for white trash."

Grandma Dee took us in knowing we weren't going to be the easiest kids to raise. And there were times we wanted to get caught, just for the attention.

Russell smacked his hand on the bar.

"That's the spirit," he yelled. "Pissing in the wind confidence. Hell-mother-fucking-yeah."

Bighead said, "Cool it," but Russell wasn't good at taking orders.

"What's that, fatman?" Russell said, cupping his hand to his ear.

"Are you looking for trouble?" Bighead asked. His cheeks were red, and I knew shit was about to go sideways.

Russell raised his hands in the air as if he was about to surrender.

"Something don't feel right," Russ said. "I can feel it in my joints."

I headed for the door, saying, "This is horse shit."

Russ twisted on his stool, hopping to his feet. He

clapped his hands. "You don't want to stay for the end of the party?"

Bighead said, "No one's leaving till I get paid."

"What'd you say?"

"Don't care if it's you or your scumbag brother, but somebody owes me twelve bucks."

Love of self. For years, I wanted to aspire to that. I went to therapy. I tried to exorcise my demons. I even learned to meditate.

But all that went out the window when shit really got real.

Russ grabbing an empty bottle of Mich Light and pitching it against the wall. Brown stars of glass sparkling in the air. I'd seen it a hundred times, but it was always slightly beautiful. That first moment of chaos was bigger than everything. It was pure, and to see something in its purest form seemed like a miracle.

But then the beast of chaos swallowed everything—the miracle included. And then it all turned ugly, which was exactly when Bighead grabbed a baseball bat behind the bar. Right pinky over left index finger. Russ read the room and wound up, pitching a second bottle right at Bighead. Chin music, announcers called it.

So I did what I always did and saved Russell from himself. Kicked a chair in front of Bighead's clown feet. His eyes were locked on Russ, so he toppled straight at him, but Russ mistook the false lunge as a threat, and Russ hit him too fast—a rabbit punch to the forehead. Bighead smacked his big head on a table as he fell, cutting his ear, which poured a stream of blood like a river. There was no justice here. That was how fine of a line it was between justice and mayhem.

But Bighead was muttering, "Russell Travers," over and over.

"You don't know us," I said.

"You're his brother."

I grabbed his head with both hands, and I wanted to smash it on the floor. Smack it over and over until he couldn't say my name anymore. Is this who I was? I couldn't tell where Russell's nightmare started and mine ended. I saw the whole thing like I was watching television. They were my hands, and that was his blood. Russ grabbed my arm and jerked at me like he was tearing my shoulder off.

I dropped Bighead's head like it was infested with cholera.

"We got to go," he said. "*Pronto.*"

I pushed into the passenger seat like I was trying to disappear, and Russ swung the truck almost sideways onto the county road. He lit a cigarette.

"Is this real?" I asked.

I had no idea what was going to set him off or sober him up. He held his cigarette out the window, the flash of cherry burning bright before disintegrating.

"I know we got our differences, but you're my only family," he said.

I'd tried to leave him before; somehow it never happened for long.

"I can't," was all I could say.

"Swing by the house tomorrow," he said. "I need a favor."

"Can't," I repeated.

"Won't ask for nothing else."

The night played out in fast-forward. Grandma Dee's house was silent, but I moved with the still night air across the kitchen, up the stairs, and into bed. The same rush and guilt and terror of my past. I could wake up to a police cruiser's red strobe light on the street, I knew that; but I fell asleep fast and dreamed of a million red apples in an orchard. From such heights, they could be all the stars in the universal. And every single one was just out of reach.

Russ raised a few pigs, and we looked over his pen. The pigs chomped at their mud underfoot. One was twice the size of the others. Bald like a crotchety old man. The sky was clear; it would be a good day to be arrested.

"Benjamin Button's the winner," Russ said, and clapped. A one-man standing ovation.

I said, "You want me to hold her, and you do the rest?"

Russ ducked into his shed, returned with a rusty knife, the blade as dull as a strip of bark.

"You don't think the rifle would be more humane?"

"You want to pull the trigger," he asked, "or does Button gets eight inches of U.S. steel?"

We separated the pigs into the overflow pen. The first time, Russ said, as soon as he slit a pig's neck the others went into a frenzy, sucking at the blood the moment it hit the mud. They fed until they found the source, and then they ate a ring through that dying pig's head.

Russell handed me his .22.

Looking to the road, I waited for the caravan of police cruisers. Why weren't they here yet?

I shouldered the .22, and he said, "Anytime today, *Kimosabi*."

Button stared after the barrel. Breathe in, hold, and squeeze the trigger. That was how you did it to keep the sight steady. A mantra for life. Always keep steady. But that wasn't my life. Growing up here, you had to move to survive. That was why I left all those years ago.

But I was pulled back, and the past slipped under my skin, burrowing deep into my core. Breathe in, hold, and I popped a shot into her head.

It wasn't uncommon for pigs to kick before they fell, but she charged, slamming my leg. Knocked me to the ground, then ricocheted headfirst into the fence. I slipped in the mud but scrambled to my feet. Russell yelped, half-laughing. The other pigs sprinted wild, back and forth. Blood-hungry. Button's face was a suck-wound, eyeball hanging loose and flapping at the end of a strand of muscle. She pinballed from one railing to the next until she dropped and squirmed in the mud. When she found purchase again, I let off another round but shot her ear clean off.

"Let me give it to her," Russell said, hopping the fence.

He bear-hugged Button and sawed at her neck with the rusty knife, the pig screaming like a hysterical child, blood caking his hands. He sawed halfway through the pig's neck before her head finally sagged.

"That's fucking awful," I said, panting, hands planted on my knees.

"No worse than the movies," he said, face and chest thick with blood. "She seem scared to you?"

"Are you shitting me?"

"If she's scared, there's a chance the meat's spoiled," he said, wiping the rusty knife on his blue jeans. "Let's get her cleaned up."

I didn't know what to expect inside his trailer. The floor was swept clean. The cupboards freshly painted yellow just like at Grandma Dee's. His rice and sugar and flour were labeled in Bell jars, lined neatly on the counter. A photograph of us as children hung on the wall, next to a photo of Mom and Dad, maybe a year or two before they left, and another old-timey one of Grandma and Grandpa on a beach before they had any kids. Then there was one final picture of Russ when he was still in high school, standing alone next to a tree. He looked away from the camera, like he was seeing into some dark future. I wasn't sure either one of us saw all this coming.

I pointed at the picture of Mom and Dad.

"Think we could be like them? Have kids and all that?"

"I was watching this movie about a guy who climbs mountains without any rope," Russ said. "There's people who climb mountains and some go to war, and others have kids. There's not much people can't do these days if they put their mind to it."

"Seems like a lot to handle though, doesn't it?"

"Kids raise themselves," Russ said. "We did okay."

I said, "I don't know; I guess. Least I had you. Maybe I'm just wanting someone to give me a set of instructions."

"I ain't going nowhere," Russ said, and poured two mugs of hot water, then stirred in instant coffee.

We took our time.

Last night, Trooper Nowack drove up in what seemed like no time; but today, after the bar incident, there's nothing—no action. Just a clock ticking down.

Russ set the sugar jar on the table. Bloody fingerprints on the glass, but I wiped them away with my sleeve.

Russ said, "I'm here, baby brother. Right now. What do you need? What can I do for you?"

"Honestly?"

"I could get you the finest smoked bacon you've ever had if you're sticking around."

"I was thinking you could stop," I said. "All the nonsense, you know?"

He seemed genuinely surprised. "Nonsense," he said, trying the word out for himself. He picked at his teeth with his fingernail and sucked something off the end. "You think someone teaches you how to climb a mountain without a rope? Think about it for a second, because if he falls, there ain't no one there to catch him. And if he does it alone, which he does, he can't take nobody down with him."

"There was no one else to bail you out last night," I said.

He laughed and brought our empty mugs to the sink.

"You never needed me, did you? I always thought I was the one helping you out. Shit, I think I convinced you of it for a good bit of time too. But I'm glad you come by."

"I can come by more," I said. "But things gotta change."

He held out his hand.

"I need some shuteye before the late shift. Tell Gram I love her."

"You too," I said, and we left it at that.

I cooked scrambled eggs for Grandma Dee. Slice of butter on top. Told her me and Russ would keep in touch, even if I knew it wasn't true. Then I took her to Walmart, St. Stanislaus church, and her senior citizen's meeting before I dropped her off at home. There was always a back road to the places we were going. Through small town after small town. Each one had its own version of me and Russell.

Driving to the airport, I listened to a radio show about security guards granted police power to handle antisocial behavior. It would only be a matter of time before I got a phone call about Russell in jail, again. It could be happening right now.

The speed limit changed from forty-five to thirty-five. In some strange way, it all seemed like the same road. There were peeling yellow houses, trailer parks, stomped flowers and cigarette butts, and abandoned cars and trucks.

Someday, they'd clean up all the mess, and this place would reset. And that was when I knew no cops were coming. Not for Russ. Not for me. Because of justice. Bighead said nothing to no one, because he was the one coming. That was life here. Every man for himself.

I pulled onto the shoulder and swung the car around. I relied on Russ, and he relied on me. The speed limit slowed to twenty-five, but I was pushing sixty in no time.

About Future

WHEN OUR MOTHER asks why I had my brother put down, I don't lie, not over the phone. "I had to," I say. "It was time."

I expect her protest: "A health issue? Was he sick?"

"He was 39," I say, like age is reason enough.

"But our family lives forever," she says. "Your great-grandmother was 96."

I know she is right, but I have to live with my decision.

"He wasn't happy," I say. "He put on a lot of weight. Had no girlfriend, nothing. There's no sense letting him suffer."

"But," she says, and there is fear in her pause, her future plans crumbling: those few good years of retirement in Florida, walking her dogs, watching cable news.

I might've even offered her our spare room, but her politics were too extreme. She'd be so much work: cooking her oatmeal for breakfast, changing her sheets, someday diapers. A nursing home would be perfect but far too expensive. And don't forget hospice. I'm a better son than to leave her with strangers.

"Plus, we never talked," I tell my mother. "He was so lonely. And 100 seems to be the new 80."

I can almost imagine the look on her face: heavy cheeks, lip shaking.

"But we don't talk much either," she says. "What about my future?"

And I say what I have to, to squelch her fears.

"I should visit soon," I say. "I can take care of you too."

Modern Lovers

THE PORCH LOOKED empty, but when I opened the screen door, a man rushed at me, arms raised.

That's what I'd told the jury. They'd questioned me for what seemed like days. A surgeon who took the stand said the bullet had entered the man's abdomen, burst his spleen, and lodged between his seventh and eighth vertebrae. The jury determined I couldn't be charged with any wrongdoing as the act was declared self-defense. The man survived, but he wasn't going to walk right ever again. Social media interpreted the event differently because the man who was trying to attack me was doing so with a very large carrot that he'd stolen from Safeway only an hour earlier. Everybody with an opinion screamed about our country's failure to help those with mental illnesses, that people like me had no tolerance for the less fortunate. But I'd sworn he had a steak knife covered in what I thought was fresh blood, though it was only the carrot's hue turned reddish under the dim porch light. My testimony, however farfetched, was convincing enough and nine out of twelve jury members determined it was a no-fault case. Reports showed that the man was not mentally ill but high on a psychedelic called Gator Grip. Apparently, the drug made you feel like you were drowning. I didn't know what people saw in it, except it made you think that every second was your last one alive. I guess there's something beautiful about that.

That was the start of a pretty bad year for me, but I won't say that the shooting led directly to anything that followed. There was only one common denominator that linked me to all those events. Me.

About the only good thing during that time in my life was Ash. Ash and I were together for three years, but I had no money most of the time because people remember the bad things a lot longer than any good thing. Employers were scared to the bone that I was going to drag some kind of drama from the shooting to the job, which seemed too big of a risk to take.

But I was a survivor, like Ash. That was one of the only things we truly had in common.

Ash told me that when she was a little girl, the electricity regularly cut out in her house in the wintertime. She said one time she woke up to her pet fish Captain Horse dead because the heat went off in the middle of the night. An ice cube, really, with a fishy center. Her father had taught her a life lesson that morning. He said plainly that when you get cold enough, you die.

Her father, coincidentally, died a few years later when his shanty dropped through the ice while he was fishing on the Sacandaga Lake. One time I heard some guy on the radio say, "We all live some; we all die some." I never figured out how you could die just some. But after Ash and I split, it made a little more sense.

FROM the bluffs, Madi and I could see the entire city. Ash was pregnant with Madi when she was only eighteen, an entire lifetime before I met her; and Madi was now almost seven. The sky was empty save the moon, but the city lights burned like stars on the streets. This was weeks after Ash left, but she was in a pinch for a sitter. She knew I could use the money, even though I told her I wouldn't take anything from her.

"Everything okay at the house?" I asked Madi. "Your momma okay?"

"All the stars are gone," Madi said, looking into the dark, dark sky.

I said, "People got greedy and wished every one away."

Barefoot, she dug her toes into the dirt and pulled at the grass.

"But they'll come back?" Madi asked. She was a sweet girl.

"You can see 'em in your head, can't you?" I said, and I figured I should take a lesson from Ash's daddy and tell this sweet little girl that the world was only as evil as you make it. "Remember your grandpa and your Uncle Lou? Just imagine 'em and the stars and anything you want, and they'll never disappear."

"Never?" she asked, twisting a strand of grass. She looked just like Ash.

I imagined the stars, my own father, and those summer nights fishing for pike with him. It took my entire life to understand that no one ever dies in your mind. That's the trouble with memories.

"Someday you'll tell your own daughter about the things in your head," I said, wanting to say more.

We watched the starless sky, and I thought that it was the only truth there was.

THE next woman I ever loved was Gina Diane. We met drinking Mad Dog out back of the bowling alley after league night. I can't say my life was any better or worse, because after Ash and Madi moved across the country, I didn't feel much of anything; my doctor had a lot to do with that. At the bowling alley, I had rolled a 280, which wasn't my best, but I was still shooting for a perfect game. Seemed like a good thing to live for. In the parking lot, Gina Diane was sitting cross-legged, itty-bitty skirt hiked high, with a guy I knew, a floorer. She tossed gravel against the concrete wall. Floorers were a type I never got. Not like welders or duct workers. You need some know-how for that. But floors, you don't even need to be literate.

A bug zapper hung off the exit sign, and it struck lightning here and there while those two sat a couple feet apart in the dark. I went out to smoke, and when I opened the door, they stopped doing what they were doing.

"Need something, man?" the floorer said.

"Do I know you?" I asked. I'd seen him on a few jobs,

way back too, from all-county football in high school. I said, "Cobleskill High, right? Full back?"

He said, "State champs three years straight."

"I played tailback for Renbrook High," I said.

"You mean Redneck High?" the floorer asked.

"I went to Renbrook," Gina Diane said. "What year?"

I said, "1998."

She said, "Jesus, boy. I could be your mother."

I said, "I do need a good mommy sometimes," and smiled.

"Why don't we make this twosome a threesome?" Gina Diane asked the floorer.

The floorer said, "Fucking inbreds," and he left.

We shared her bottle of Mad Dog 20/20, and she told me her biggest fear was that she'd die in a gutter, people driving by without helping her.

I said, "Why would you be in a gutter?"

She said, "Where else would I sleep if I couldn't drive home?"

I said, "You're no lady, but you're all right."

She said, "Now you tell me a secret you never told nobody."

"I shot a man," I said. "But that's no secret."

"You're funny," she said. "What's your name again?"

"That'll be the secret, how about?" I said, and we each drank.

"I let my uncle touch me once," she said, and laughed. "I'm only kidding. It was twice."

I choked on the drink, and we both laughed hard. Then I kissed her; maybe she kissed me.

I⟨T⟩ wasn't long after that she was pregnant. Gina Diane and I were living together, and she said she was nervous because she was going on forty. The doctor had said the blood wasn't abnormal, but he said to keep an eye out. I remember not that long ago that I was going down this exact same road with Ash saying we wouldn't do to our kids what our folks did to us. I remember because it was all talk, hypothetical, but now, for the first time in my life, I thought maybe I did want a kid.

W⟨E⟩ had shopping to do. Weekend yard sales, and not in the poor places either, but in the neighborhoods with mailboxes with nameplates and two-car garages. They sold a fancy dream.

We looked at a kid's blue dresser, some girls' names in black marker written down the backside. Some little dipshit, I imagined, writing Sandy and Amanda, like he would have options when he got old enough.

Gina Diane held a pair of black Levi's to her waist. They were the kind she used to wear. Tight in the ass. Low on the hips. But she folded them, setting them back.

"They look good," I said.

"Those days are plenty over," she said.

I picked up a raggedy doll with red hair and spoke out the side of my mouth.

"Come on, girlie," I said. "Let Daddy buy 'em for you."

"Don't be an idiot," she said, smiling like the first time we met.

When I was nine, my father sat me down at the kitchen table, his suitcase packed. The buckles were broken, but he cinched the bag shut with a bungee cord from his truck.

"When you shoot one bird flying, you shoot all the birds flying," my father had said.

"What does that mean?" I had asked.

My father had nodded at me, but he didn't smile. "Means the last woman you meet is as good as the first one."

And now I knew just how true that was.

SINCE high school, Billy and I had been coming to Tiny's garage nearly every weekend. Billy hung a turkey from the rafters. Its body half-skinned, hide pulled down like a sock. Condensation beaded on our Busch cans. Billy was back from West Virginia buying fireworks, selling M-80s and Blackcats to scrubs behind the Fuel-n-Food. The Yankee game crackled from the radio, and Tiny and some asshole were out front working on the F-150 Tiny bought at the police auction.

I leaned against the welding bench. "It really as back-woods as they say?" I asked.

Billy shook his head, slicing through turkey fat, yanking skin from muscle. "Third world, maybe. A lot more than here. Like, I saw a pet deer."

"As a real pet?" I asked.

"Behind some dude's house. Real beautiful eyes. That's what he was trying to sell me after I bought up a bunch of his fireworks. Eyes you'd want to look at while making love."

"Who the hell makes love to a deer?" I asked. "Everybody knows you just fuck 'em."

Billy scratched his neck, his knuckles covered in blood and hunks of white fat. "That's how you got yourself in your damn predicament, huh?"

"Shit's real, I guess." I grabbed a handful of screws from a coffee can, tossing them back one by one.

Out front, we heard a loud metal crash, and Tiny called what's-his-name a shitbag, and they both howled.

"Really, though," I said. "I wish I could do it all over. Stuff I know now would've been nice ten years ago."

"With Gina?" he asked.

"With Ash," I said. "I'd a told her to go to the damn door that night. Let that crazy dude with the fucking carrot stab her in the face."

Billy laughed, drawing his blade across the turkey's thigh, leaving a slug of blood and slapped the blade shut. He gave a final yank to the hide, and the turkey was all pink and muscly.

Billy said, "That's some shit, man. I thought you loved that girl."

"Me too," I said. "That's part of the problem, I guess."

I finished my beer, crushed the can. I really wanted to tell Billy that I thought staying together with Gina Diane was bad news; anyone could see that. Or maybe I knew that she'd run off someday, and it'd be me and the kid, and in twenty years that kid would turn out to be like me, and that's a lot of misery for something so pure and good as your own blood. *Why wait to break her heart*, I thought. Everybody would heal better.

"If things ever got bad at home, you think I could crash on your couch for a couple nights?" I asked.

"You're talking to the wrong person if you're already thinking about leaving her. Jesus, man."

"Yeah," I said, opening another beer.

"I mean, you ain't no better than every other piece of shit in this town," Billy said, then he admired the skinned bird's slick, hard muscles. But he nodded slowly. "Sure. Whatever," he said. "Stay as long as you want."

"Maybe just one night," I said, and I wasn't sure if I felt better or worse.

EVERY light was off in the trailer, but the front door was open, TV going. News about protests in New York City; a cop shot a twelve-year-old boy who pointed a toy gun at him.

Gina Diane was breathing real quiet in the bedroom, but I knew she wasn't sleeping. I knocked my knee against the edge of the bed.

I stripped naked, said, "Go back to sleep."

In bed, she trembled when I pressed against her. Her breath reeked sweetly, like booze.

I said, "You're not supposed to be drinking."

"It's cough medicine," she said.

The first night we met, behind the bowling alley, we daydreamed. "In a year," I'd told her, "I'll be working regular. Jobs always pick up in the summer, and we'll buy Heineken. Take weekends off too." She said she was quitting cold turkey, meetings, twelve steps, all that. Then we drank all her Mad Dog and talked about the peppers and squash we'd plant someday in the garden. About the name of our first dog and firstborn.

But the future was entirely different. I wrapped the pillow around my face

I said, "I don't know if I can do this."

"What?" she said. "Christ, what did you say?"

"I don't know about seeing things through," I said. "About signing up for more."

"You know what you sound like?" she asked. "Because I know every excuse from every guy in this town."

I tried to remember that bronzed, drunken feeling I felt with her at the bowling alley or those mornings when I was a kid and my mother fixed *Cream of Wheat* on the stove and swore that Dad leaving was going to be the best thing for everyone. I wasn't either of those people anymore, and I had no idea how to be start being someone better.

The bedroom was quiet and mostly dark, but straws of blonde light bordered the windows. Somewhere out there was the moon, or just a streetlamp. Either way, light rained down, trying to get in.

Dracula Mountain

THEY CALLED IT Dracula Mountain. The stony peak—
rock like metal in the hard sun—cresting clouds. The crows
cawing from the shadows, and that smell of ammonia
choking every sense.

Then Carter, up the trail, staggered toward us. Lost for
how long now? Seventeen years old, but pale and skeletal. Back from the dead. Bit by the beast, the story went.
Harmon Barley, my Lizzie's brother, said he saw the whole
thing. "A creature with six-foot wings. Flew right out from
the tree, grabbing him by the shoulders. Yanked him out
of his own shoes." Carter's body supposedly fell to the
ground, his arms and chest bit up. Gasping for air. Harmon left him for dead, but here Carter was, alive as the day
he was born.

Harmon Barley was known to lie when it served him,
but his sister Lizzie said, "Nightwalkers been around for
eons, and it was only a matter of time before they take this

world back." Dozens had disappeared before Carter, but only a few had come back to us. They all had the same bite marks, and they were quarantined. Incisors and canines extracted for safety.

Lizzie never lost hope that her boy was still out there. We searched the mountain for months. If the creatures didn't have him, starvation certainly did. I never said this to Lizzie because I liked her company, and now that she says she loves me, I owe it to her to keep looking.

In the beginning we were happy, mostly. Lizzie sold insurance, and I dreamed of sailing to Central America if I could ever save enough. She was on a work trip to Iowa when Carter went missing. Neighbors saw nothing but agreed one hundred percent she should have never left him alone. I stopped by once when she wasn't home. Dark, deep pockets under his eyes. He blinked uncontrollably. "Allergies," Carter lied. He was a mess who was always going to be a mess, but Lizzie was a good mom. If I'd have known I'd be searching for him night after night and her waking up screaming and crying out for him, I'd have handcuffed him in the basement with a bowl of water like a dog. Then he'd never break her heart.

Before the stories of monsters and before she said she loved me, the town had another problem. When the paper mill shuttered, people overloaded on uppers to work two or three part-time jobs to pay their mounting bills. They couldn't afford the pace. They needed cheaper, stronger drugs, and a slew of underground concoctions were born. I heard stories of kids experimenting with their own recipes. The vilest of them burned through their veins like pure acid. Loose meat like slow-cooked brisket hanging off their bones.

The world got dark fast. And people quit living for any good future. Before we knew it, they were vanishing completely, including Lizzie's boy.

When we found Carter, he could barely walk. Arms violent with pustules. I grabbed Lizzie from hugging him on the trail. "But he's my baby," she pleaded. I wrapped him in a blanket and carried him all the way downhill.

Before first light, Lizzie was finally asleep. Carter was in his own bed, moaning and babbling. *He'll be fine*, I told myself, but I could hear him on the phone. I pushed my palms against my temples. That unbearable conversation. "I need it," he repeated. "I'll kill somebody, I don't care." If he didn't tear us apart before, it was only a matter of time. The certainty of it helped me to my feet. I pushed open his door, said, "Get up." Grabbing his face, his lips opened to speak, I forced all the cash I had saved for that sailboat and that bullshit dream into that black pit of a mouth. I said, "If you ever come back, I'll live forever to make your life hell." He gripped the cash and breathed out slowly—calm, proud. I was a monster, but to him, I was nothing but a savior.

Saturday Night Special

THE DEBUTANTE SMELLED like sex. Twenty-eight degrees and snowing in the city, but in Wayne's pickup, the heat blew hard, and the dome light burned orange and bright. The windows were fogged, save a five-toed footprint on the windshield. The Debutante applied peach lipstick and sprayed Tommy Girl on her neck; then she licked a smear of color off her teeth. Wayne signaled down Canal Road. Driving along the Moohocken River, moonlight reflected from the ice. Wayne pinched the welt beneath his eye. The Debutante had asked how it happened, and he said, "When you mess with a bull, sometimes you get the horns," and she nodded like she knew all about bulls. Wayne liked her well enough until she asked to get paid.

"What do you mean you got no money?" Her hand shook as she lit a Newport and drew from the cigarette. "You ain't got no ethics? It's called fair exchange."

"I'll get it," Wayne said.

"Fuck right you will!" she said. "'Cause I don't work for free. This ain't no Peace Corps."

In his periphery, he saw brick walls and alley-gaps passing. He play-ignored her, the way ego-hurt children do. Only twenty inches separated them, but he did not hear a word.

"My pussy makes money," she said.

"I got plenty of ethics," Wayne said, and shifted gears.

EARLIER in the evening, Wayne had walked from Slider's Pool Hall to his Ford, a stolen cue stick in hand. The pool hall management never said they were sorry or refunded his table fee. Wayne's pocket should've bulged with his winnings. Still, he grinned over his last shot. He was eighteen but shot like a young Efren Reyes, who was considered the best in the world. People back home in Galway even called Wayne by Reyes' nickname, "The Magician," and it stuck, especially since he had won the Galway Nine-ball Classic two of the last three years. In Albany, though, nobody knew his name.

At Slider's, overhead lamps had shined down on each table, perfect for pool, no distracting shadows. The room held twelve tables, four rows of three, with green felt as rich as smooth meadow-grass in the country. No jukebox meant no honky-tonk, no hip-hop, no rock and roll. No gospel, no blues. No folk, no nothing. Just the thunderous sounds of pool balls smacking, the clack-clock of each collision. Wayne kept to the corner tables, staying out of sight. Abide the hustler's code. Use a "house" cue stick. Show you're vulnerable, unthreatening, even broken. Because sharks know sharks.

After he had dumped three small-stakes games to prove he wasn't in fact a hustler, he played a local jean jacket with a ponytail for fifty dollars a ball. Wayne shattered the perfect diamond on the break, sending the two-ball in the side and the eight in the corner.

"Holy hell," Wayne said.

"Not bad, shooter," said Ponytail.

Wayne cupped his hand to his ear. "What's that?" He pointed at the side of his head. "This ear's fucked. Exhaust went off like a shotgun when I was under my truck. Blew my drum to shit."

Ponytail cleared his throat. "We gonna talk cars or shoot pool?"

"Right," Wayne said.

Since the group home experience, Wayne had had enough with adults telling him what to do or how to act. This city didn't know The Magician, but they should. Wayne called a wild one-seven-nine combo and Ponytail laughed, dismissing him like Wayne was a kid wishing on a shooting star, a pipedream shot, but that was that, because click-clack-click, *thuunk*. The nine-ball sunk into the corner pocket. Wayne let his arms go slack at his sides, a move of surprise he'd perfected and performed a hundred times, with a look of awe on his face, big-dumb-eyed and stunned.

"Look at that now," Wayne said.

He plucked the folded money from the table, and he exhaled loudly, play-acting as if the awful shots and other

down-and-out-piss-poor-good-for-nothing-bad-choices and
even worse outcomes were behind him. But the truth was,
Wayne was still on the upswing, riding the unexplainable
inertia of a winning streak. He had hopped on Interstate
87 out of Lake George a few weeks ago with nearly $400
in his wallet and Saratoga with another $600. In Fonda
he pocketed $150, and in Broadalbin he counted out the
night with ten crisp twenties.

"I'd never mind that money," Ponytail said, eyeing the
bills in Wayne's hand.

Ponytail and two more hulks like him—tall, denim-clad,
and barrel-thick—backed Wayne up near a payphone on the
wall.

"You're a fucking cheat," Ponytail said.

"Fucking lucky," Wayne said. "Never shot so good in my
whole life."

"You really deaf in this ear?"

Wayne felt a pair of hands wrestle the money away and
another set of hands pin his shoulders to the wall. They
told him never to show his face in Slider's or they'd cut
him from ass to mouth. Raised in the country, Wayne's
father had shown him how to dress a deer properly, cutting
from just above the genitals to the rib cage. Wayne wanted
to laugh at these city people and his lips curled, revealing
dimples like knife-slits deep in his cheeks.

Wayne said, "This how you treat your boyfriend?" and
Ponytail—without hesitating—coldcocked Wayne in the jaw
with the payphone. A lightning-white flash burst behind
his eyelids. A shock of white stars, like in a cartoon strip.

The two others held Wayne by the armpits to keep him from dropping to his knees, and Ponytail popped Wayne flush in the eye with the speaker of the phone, the clack of plastic against bone. The gang tossed him into the back alley with the trashcans. Fire escapes dangled overhead. The men kicked Wayne as he staggered to his unsure feet. A cue stick thumped hard against his back, but he turned fast and wrenched it away. All young legs and scared, he ran hard. He heard them cussing—*cocksucker this* and *cocksucker that.* Wayne knew the stories of hustlers getting busted. Broken arms. Broken skulls. Worse.

But this was his lucky day. Only a few scratches. A puffy eye. He even had a "house" cue to pair with the tournament stick in his truck.

Wayne spotted his Ford at the far end of the avenue. Neon lights lit the sidewalks in an electric haze: yellow, pink, white. The buzzing and humming of commerce. *Sale. Cold Beer. XXX. ATM.* Shouts from toughies and whores and punks and posers, negotiating and catcalling. And all that rough laughter. Noise blood of the city.

Metal newspaper boxes lined the corners, the cover story of the self-proclaimed national terrorist group, the Animal Liberation Movement of America, who had broken into the zoo, cutting locks and spilling into the heart of the city all those caged beasts—tigers, gazelles, two red wolves, and a zebra—now all roaming the wild winter streets. Wayne figured some would freeze by morning. Maybe the Animal Liberation Movement knew that, or maybe it was that eight hours of freedom in the city was better than a lifetime in a cage. Wayne had heard that a twelve-foot alligator was found under a taxi on Jefferson Drive, but it was a separate incident. The city was the new jungle.

Wayne's keys jangled in his hand, a hairless rabbit foot hanging from the key ring. He punched the crosswalk signal and waited at the corner with the working girls, the women wearing faux fur and loud colors, costumes you'd see in Halloween stores. Red stockings. Purple blouses. Leopard-print skirts. Their lips were blue from cold.

A bus stopped, and a Cadillac Escalade burned a red light, blowing its horn like Hallelujah.

The Debutante crossed the street toward Wayne, and he guessed she still had two years before she was legal. She carried a glitter-gold shoulder purse with spaghetti straps. The streetlamps shined against her curly helmet of hair, dark and full like a fat blackberry. She smoked a Newport, the cherry blazing like a traffic light. Her face was squared-off, like a piece of caramel, fat cheeks and a wide jaw, but a body like a young boy's. Five feet two inches tall. Ninety-eight pounds. She bit her fingernail till it bled. She probably told her girlfriends some guys liked her fingers in their ass. She would say she didn't mind either if it made them cum quicker.

She called out all sweet to Wayne—*baby this* and *baby that.*

"Baby. Warm me up, baby." She bit her lip.

"I'm married, cutie pie," he lied.

He'd only had one girlfriend in all his life. Dee. That was at the group home when they were both seventeen.

Dee's father had been arrested on insurance fraud charges, caught claiming the house basement flooded thirteen times in four years. Her mother divorced him for Dee's boss, Brad Jennings, of Jennings Grocery Store, where Dee worked as a bagger. Hearing the news, Dee acted out and cut at her juvenile thighs with a razor blade, a series of hidden tick-marks near her underwear line, eighteen incisions in all, but then just stopped. So she said. Like that time she smoked meth. A one-time deal. But her mother noticed them one morning as she stood in their fogged-up bathroom complaining of Jennings's bad breath and chubby fingers and missing her husband and whatever else she could think of. Dee stepped from the shower, and her mother howled at the tiny red cuts.

"Haven't I taught you nothing? Who's gonna love you all cut up like pork?"

Dee was sent upstate to the Covenant Home for Boys and Girls, an outreach center, where she met another first-timer, an under-aged boy arrested for stealing his father's pickup truck for joyrides to the city. A judge had required Wayne to spend three weeks in treatment. Because they were new, their shyness brought them together, sitting quietly beside one another during meals and meetings. They were both pimply but lean-bodied, with straight teeth and cleft chins, like siblings.

During free time in the common room, Wayne and Dee cut up magazines to collage while a cartoon movie played for the others. Two counselors monitored the teens. Dee confessed to Wayne that she only cut herself because she was bored. That's why she did most things. She had won a scholarship to the university. She had a good life, she'd said.

"But I want more." Her eyes were still bloodshot from crying that morning. "Don't you?"

Wayne wanted to kiss her.

"I guess I want to swim in the ocean," he said.

"I hate sharks!" she said. "Don't you want to meet movie stars? If we had a car, we could run away." She leaned close and whispered, "I could be your girlfriend."

"Boundaries," a counselor said. "Both of you, back to the movie."

After three weeks, they were sent home, and Wayne stole his father's pickup. He and Dee drove west. At a Texaco Station outside of Oneonta, Wayne spent four dollars in a gumball machine until he won a plastic engagement ring.

"I'll buy you a real one too," he said.

They walked down the candy aisle holding hands. Dee slid a MoonPie into her pocket.

On their way out, she dropped a quarter into the gumball machine and won an eyeball sticker and stuck it to Wayne's forehead.

"So you can find your way home," she said.

"To you," he said.

She shook her head.

"I don't want to hurt you, but sometimes I do stupid shit," she said.

In Binghamton, where Dee had friends, she had convinced him to rent a room at the Super 8. Above the bed hung a three-foot painting of a lighthouse on a rocky beach. Dee laid on the comforter, her arms wide and legs apart.

"I'm like that drawing. You know that one where the guy looks like he's making a snow angel?" She laughed. "You know what would be fun?"

She said she knew a dealer, Christo, in the area who sold meth.

"You've gotta try it. You'll see the face of God," she said. "But even more, too. You'll, like, see God's pores."

"How much?" Wayne asked.

She pulled him onto the bed and pushed her tongue into his ear. "It's all on me," she said. "How about you go buy us snacks while I call Christo. Get me some cookies."

Wayne drove to the Shell Station. He bought a quart of milk and a bag of Oreos. He had been gone thirty minutes and returned to her naked from the waist down on the bed, her eyes as big as coffee saucers. The toilet flushed and out from the bathroom walked Christo with tattoo sleeves on each arm, the ink faces of a dozen babies. The man never glanced at Wayne, just eased Dee's knees apart and laid on top of her. The quart of milk broke open when it hit the floor. Dee's head turned, but Wayne knew she wasn't looking at him. Standing in the milk puddle, he gripped his keys until the metal teeth cut into his palm.

He never saw her again.

BUT back in the wild, beating city the candy Debutante said, "Baby, if you're married you can take your wedding ring off if it'd make you feel better, baby."

"Pussies wear rings," Wayne said.

"And you're not, right, baby?" she asked. "No cop either, right, baby?"

His pockets were empty, but he wasn't going home. He'd been on the road for six months, and lately he'd won big and had been buying himself dinners at the Olive Garden and sleeping on queen-sized beds in Motel 6s.

"Right, baby," he said. "I'm definitely no cop."

In the bridge district, Wayne parked his pickup beneath construction scaffolding. Surrounding them, a carpet factory, a furniture warehouse, and abandoned, boarded buildings. Dark. Industrial. Perfect for crime. It was a full moon night, and light refracted off the frozen river that ran through the city as if the entire surface was mercurial. She told him her name was Carlotta. She had come to the city to be a dancer. Wayne was never much of a dancer, but his grandmother had often told him when he was a boy that he had piano fingers.

"I'm going to learn to play before she dies," Wayne said. "One of these days. Not that she's going to die soon or nothing."

The heater fan blew hard, and Wayne rubbed his hands together. Carlotta told him that he was one of the good ones and that she needed to break her cycle of all those bad ones that had come before. She liked his face and told him that too, and he walked his piano fingers up her thigh and called her a real sweet thing. She let him kiss her mouth, and they were both cold but wrestled their pants to their knees. Wayne fumbled with a condom, and the moment he pushed into her, he came and buried his face into her neck.

"It's okay, baby," she whispered. "Everybody cums."

But then she asked to get paid.

Wayne figured there were consequences if Carlotta showed up without her payday. He imagined her recollecting some worker's manual. Learn the book. Memorize the scenarios. Score at least an 85 percentile on the final exit-exam. All procedural, like in the vocational class he'd taken his junior year. What do you do in this situation?

Flip to the Trouble-Shooting Index.

Find, *If a client (A.K.A. "the John") does not/cannot pay for services requested.*

Go to Page 52.

Failure to Pay for Vaginal Intercourse.

First, raise voice at client to demonstrate authority. Use the imperative mood. Include profanity as necessary. (For example: *Pay me, cheap motherfucker!*)

Second, verbally threaten client. This may be by way of physical violence or death inflicted by the escort or escort's procurer/procuress (A.K.A. *"Pimp"*).

Third, if verbal threats appear ineffective, resort to concealed weapon (see *Self-Defense*).

Carlotta ran through each step with a passion Wayne had only witnessed a few times in his life. It reminded him of his mother, all red-faced and spitting mad. Like when Wayne was twelve years old and his mother left the house carrying only a shoebox, and whether that shoebox was stuffed with fancy underwear or a snub-nosed pistol wrapped in newsprint, it made his father edgy until she finally came home again. His father, Emmitt, worked collections for Zeke Mickelson, a bookie in Albany. Zeke hired a lot of thick-skulled country boys, and Emmitt fit the bill to a tee. But on a run outside of Amsterdam, Emmitt was robbed. So he said. The following week, their outbuilding was set afire and a few days later, Emmitt came home with a gash on his forehead and a black eye, and whenever he swore or coughed, he held his hands against his ribs.

Wayne's mother stood in the kitchen wearing her best dress, flower-patterned and cut at the knees, holding a shoebox to her stomach.

"Mama's got to take care of some business," she said, as Wayne ate his breakfast. "But I'll be back real soon, sweet pea."

"You don't have to do this," Emmitt said, leaning against the door.

Wayne knew that if he wasn't in the room, she might go after his father with a knife.

"Zeke might not hear you, but he'll listen to what I got to say," she said.

"Don't," Emmitt said. "I can fix this."

But she pushed past him, and before dinner she was home again with no more trouble from Zeke Mickelson.

As the nightscape flickered outside the Ford's windows, Wayne had figured it all out. He'd return to Slider's. He'd gamble his tournament stick, a Lucasi, that he had won off a drifter in Poughkeepsie. It was easily worth $800. He'd lose it in game one only to win it back in game two, and in games three and four, he'd play for cash. After four games, he'd have enough scratch to pay Carlotta double and buy her a shrimp scampi dinner at Friday's.

"Give me my money," Carlotta said. "Or you're dead!"

"Marry me," Wayne said.

"Fuck yourself next time."

She pulled a knife from her glitter-gold purse (see *Self-Defense*), a single-action, out-the-front, button-lock switchblade, and gripped it like the pearl handle was cut for her palm only.

"You're goddamn crazy!"

Wayne twisted the steering wheel as he skirted her blade.

And Carlotta screamed. In that moment, a furry body broke across the headlight plain, suddenly absorbed by the white conical light. Wayne felt the impact in his hands, the jolt in the steering wheel against his palms—the lump-lump of the truck traveling across something solid. One headlight blazed, the other cracked and dim. Wayne opened the door to the sound of night. Wind scraped the concrete pillars and steel scaffolding of the bridges overhead, and the singing icy river crackled with ice jams. The parking light cast a red glow along the rutted pavement. On an iced over puddle lay a silenced wolf. A wild beast in center-city. A zoo animal. Wayne thought he was hallucinating, but he heard panting from the wolf's great long body. Its front legs twitched, but the rear were dead still. The night smelled of tin.

Hugging herself from the cold, Carlotta stood beside Wayne.

"My father gave me a Snoopy dog," she said. "But Mom left it at the park just like the parrot he got me. Said I wasn't mature enough for any pets."

"What's that have to do with anything?" Wayne asked.

"Shut up," she said. "I just mean let somebody else find it."

Wayne reached out, his fingers touching the wolf's snout when the animal jerked, its jaw springing like a trap. Wayne flinched and squeezed a fist, more cold than hurt.

"We're going to get caught," Carlotta said. "And I'm not going to jail because of some dead dog."

"Dead dogs don't bite," Wayne said.

"I'm no retard," she said, and pushed him. He yanked her arm, and she fell hard, gravel covering the sleeve of her coat. She scrambled to lift herself.

"I didn't mean it," he said.

He brushed her arm, but she pulled away.

She lit another cigarette. "It's funny, but you remind me of him."

"Who?" Wayne asked.

"My father."

"I'm trying to help here."

"He was always trying too," she said.

Wayne shook out a blanket that was stuffed behind the driver's seat and swaddled the wolf. Halfway down its back, bone splintered through the fur. The wolf whined as he dumped it in the truck bed.

"You know you got to put him down," she said. "He's sick."

Wayne wanted to tell her to shut up, but he knew she was right.

They drove in silence. Wayne steered toward the river. He thought it was a horrible way to die, but the wolf wouldn't suffer. The freezing river water was fast.

Drug dealers and prostitutes ran business under the bridge all night long, and like the addicts and thieves and fighters and hustlers, they were family. The next morning when they all laid down their weary heads, Wayne imagined he'd hear their thoughts and wishes, their tired collective breath murmuring *help me from myself, dear God, please have mercy*, and the city would again brighten with the blue-steel light of dawn as the river carried the beast away.

"I'll get your money," Wayne said. "Give me till tomorrow."

"I don't care," she said, staring out the window. "I just want to go home."

"Won't you get in trouble?" he asked. "I can take you someplace else."

"Fuck you," she said. "I mean my real home."

The river was twenty yards off. Wayne braked the truck and cut the engine. Carlotta leaned against the passenger window. She breathed quietly, evenly. A shadow fell across her cheek. Her eyes were shut like she was dreaming, so when Wayne noticed the blue and red strobe of a parked police cruiser flash in his rearview, he thought he too might have drifted off to sleep. But he heard the chirp of the siren, and he knew what his father told him all those years ago was the truth—nothing comes easy. Wayne looked at Carlotta, her sweet young face a stranger in this hard harsh city, and maybe he could love her or maybe he'd learn to. He turned the key as the engine rumbled again to life.

WHEN Wayne was thirteen years old, he and his father had built duck houses in their garage. Wayne sawed and sawed into a knotty pine board, the friction-whistle of the blade screaming hot against wood. His father told him there was no getting around some things in life, and when it got tough you had to lean in. Wayne let his weight fall into each saw stroke. His arms burned like his muscles were blood-boiled. His father yanked the saw from his hands. He spit on the blade, and Wayne heard the boiling wet sizzle. He told Wayne to hold out his palm, and Wayne yelled as his father touched the searing blade against his skin, the flesh bubbling. His father choked back his own cry, as if the blade was burning his own calloused hand.

"Don't fight it. You ain't made of nothing the world can't break," his father said. "You'll learn. And when you do, you'll thank me, son."

Sky Meets Sea

THE MAILBOX HAD been knocked down, blown-up, spray-painted, hit with rocks, hit with bricks, hit with a garbage can, and once it was filled with spoiled milk.

After two years of active duty, Frost was placed on the Individual Ready Reserve. He and Lee Marie rented a broke-down one-bedroom house in a derelict neighborhood in Amsterdam. They had met in the worst possible place on earth, all sand and burning heat and stink near Kabul, but in upstate New York, they enjoyed that clean-air smell and buzz-cut lawns and not always locking the front door at night.

Their street never had trouble, but Frost planned a stakeout to catch the mailbox vandal. At the front window, he had a clean view down the driveway, and he forked at a plate of leftover enchiladas. His thermos was topped with coffee, and a Louisville Slugger leaned by the door. Frost had wrapped the mailbox with duct tape to keep it from falling. He was working at the duct tape factory running the Jumbo cutter, and his closet at home was stuffed with trash bags of tape. But he wasn't going back to the factory. Frost knew that walking out on a job sounded bad, but Lee Marie wouldn't want to hear it, not with their bills. Lee Marie didn't want to hear a lot of things. So Frost told her he'd been laid off.

It was after midnight, and the streetlamp threw a halo around the mailbox. Frost had pulled enough overnighters to know how it was done. He chased two tabs of Desoxyn with coffee and scribbled in a notepad. Circles mostly. Endless circles.

Across the street, porch lights shined on the neighbors' shambly houses. The dark ones foreclosed. But no light shined at Bill and Seline's either. Seline's Honda was gone. She was attractive, thirty-five, a decade older than Bill and Frost, and if she left the house in sweats to go to the gym or in a black dress at eight at night, she always wore red-hot lipstick. No one else looked that good, not even the twenty-somethings that Frost ran with because they wrestled with the addictions that shed decades from their lives in a year or two. Frost used to daydream that if Seline ever left Bill, he would keep her company.

But he loved Lee Marie.

LATELY, Frost had felt like his father, a paranoid old man.

When Frost was a teenager, they built duck houses in their workshop.

"Someone's out there to get you, dummy," his father, Abe, would say.

Abe had a big head and a wide, flat face, and from a distance, he looked like a six-foot thumb.

"Think about it," Abe would say. "The world doesn't work unless you got an opposite. Like dogs and cats, or up and down."

"Like yin and yang," Frost said. "Like that?"

"Whatever," Abe said. "Just be careful, because sometimes it's the same person."

Frost held two boards together while Abe pounded a nail. The boards slipped, and Abe nailed unevenly.

"For Christ's sake. Can't you do nothing?"

Abe ripped the boards from his son, and with the claw-side of the hammer he pried the nail screaming loose.

In his youth, Abe too had served in the military as a Navy seaman, a night watchman. He had told Frost that from a ship's deck, he could stare out at the ocean, scan the horizon for the smallest anomaly, the faintest difference along that line where sky meets sea. Near dawn, his eyes played tricks. Ghost light from the early sun refracted god-knows-what and a vessel appeared. He'd swear it was an enemy ship, but almost always the shape morphed. Once he said he saw an African elephant walking on the water. He spent two long years at sea, but it only took a few short months in the wild blue nothing for him to distrust almost everything he saw.

Abe was discharged, not for his eyes but his hand, crushed beneath a pallet carrying half a dozen hundred-pound artillery shells—fallen from a forklift—as he unloaded cargo off the coast of the Panay Islands.

His left mitt resembled a ginger root. The fingers bent

upward save his pinky. Missing. The heavy load from the pallet tore it clean off. He worked as a welder for the next thirty-seven years, paid mostly under the table.

Now retired, Abe kept order at home by carrying a toy pistol, shooting caps at his ex-wife Gina's dog, a German shepherd named Missy. When she jumped on the couch, there was always a quick percussion of pops. Missy's eyebrows would raise, but her head stayed mounted on the armrest.

"Missy pissy," Abe would say.

In the kitchen, Abe set two crooked fingers on Gina's hip. She was his second wife, fifteen years his junior. She worked as a nurse on the Alzheimer's unit at St. Mary's Hospital, and after they divorced, she loved hating him. Then the hate turned to irritation and then to ambivalence. Then Abe disappeared from her thoughts altogether, and with the images of him long receded to the far corners of her mind, for a time she was happy. Abe made it crystal clear while they were married that he would not father another child. Until lately, a child was all that mattered to her. But the year of Gina's fifty-second birthday, nature made certain that she would never be a mother.

Still, she cooked Abe dinner once a month. But no longer did they argue about children.

"You'll never believe what your dog just did," Abe would say, standing near the stove, two fingers on her hip.

She would push him away.

"I was going to tell you it smells good."

"I was going to let you starve," she said. "Now quit."

1:00 A.M. Frost drew black circles in the notebook. Until last week, the duct tape factory was one hundred and five days without an accident, only twenty days from a free meat lunch.

Both Frost and Johnny Cast, a twenty-something veteran from Fort Drum, worked the Jumbo cutters. The Jumbo sliced six-foot-long rolls of duct tape into smaller sizes for stores. To Frost, the machine looked like a giant bread slicer.

Johnny Cast had returned to work after a failed drug test. Under normal circumstances, Johnny should've lost his job, but the foreman, Dunkin Daniels, was another Fort Drum vet who believed in that brotherhood that binds men of war. If Johnny committed to a drug detention center, Dunkin vowed to hold his job.

The day Johnny returned, he had handed Frost a blue cigar.

"Diaper spelled backwards is repaid," Frost had said.

"What's cocksucker spelled backwards?" Johnny asked.

"Congratulations."

"I been gone forever," Johnny said. "It's immaculate conception or some shit. But I love Izzy."

Frost had known very few men who would raise another man's child so casually. But Johnny was loyal. And as foolish as he seemed, Frost had always liked him for that.

Frost called for a celebration at Tiny's Tavern. The bar was full of twenty-year-old drunks going on forty and forty-year-old drunks at their end. But the lights were dim, and they all looked like ageless drunks. Johnny fed the jukebox ten bucks and ran through every Merle Haggard track.

"Every song's about some loser," Frost said.

"I'll drink to that." Johnny downed his shot of whiskey and sipped his beer. "It says something about the human condition."

"What the fuck does that mean?" Frost asked. "One of your counselors say that?"

He saw Johnny's eyes lose some shine.

"Means we can't all be saints," Johnny said.

Frost flagged the bartender. He ordered another pitcher and two more whiskeys.

"You know how I found out about Izzy?" Johnny asked.

Frost checked his watch, almost midnight. He had never called Lee Marie to tell her he was out.

"Limp dick, you know?" Johnny laughed to himself.

"Booze will do it," Frost said.

"Mine's mush all the time."

The bartender set down their round, and Frost stole the shot glass to his lips, the slow-burn of rotten honesty in his head.

Frost drove Johnny to a trailer park called The Lion's Den. Izzy stood inside the screen door wearing an Army tank top that hung mid-thigh. She was tiny, a hundred and five pounds, and if Frost didn't know she was pregnant, he'd think her belly distended like a wino's.

They staggered up the steps.

"I took him out to celebrate," Frost said. "It's not his fault."

"I'm a father," Johnny mumbled, drunkenly.

"You tell him who the father is?" Frost asked.

Izzy took Johnny's arm around her shoulders. Her body

gave under his weight, but she stood strong, accepting his burden.

"Let me take him to bed," Frost said.

She smiled for the first time. "You're good to him."

The bedroom was only large enough to fit a bed, a dresser, and a thrift-store bassinet. On the wall hung a metal cross and Izzy's community college diploma. Frost laid Johnny down and flapped the blankets over his legs. Johnny tried to unclasp his belt but gave up.

"My arm fell asleep," Johnny said. "Can't sleep with pants on."

Frost slid Johnny's jeans off, leaving them bundled on the floor.

"Don't get no ideas," Johnny said.

Izzy sat at the card table in the kitchen, two mugs of coffee set beside a stack of bridal magazines.

"I didn't have time to clean up," Izzy said.

"It'll just get messy again," Frost said.

"Ain't that the truth," she said. "Everything's a fucking mess."

They drank in silence and held hands.

They had never meant for it to happen.

A couple months ago, they'd bumped into each other at Tiny's Tavern. Izzy drank a glass of house red. She was meeting a girlfriend, but her girlfriend was thirty minutes late.

"Men trouble," Izzy said. "All my friends got it."

"Not you," Frost said. But with Johnny in rehab, he knew he should've kept his mouth shut.

He ordered her next wine and a whiskey and beer back.

"Can I ask you something?" Izzy said.

"I think you just did," Frost said.

She pushed his arm playfully.

"Johnny says you don't have kids."

"That comes up with Lee," Frost said. "But it ain't my choice, right?"

Izzy nodded like she knew exactly what he meant.

"My dad wasn't so good to me," Frost said. "But I think I could do better."

"I'm sorry," she said, wiping her face. "It's just Johnny ain't here, and he's got his own problems. And I really am sorry. You don't have to listen to none of this."

Frost set his hand on hers, but she pulled away.

"Let's go," Frost said. "Let me drive you home."

"I don't know," she said.

In her driveway, he tugged her onto his lap. Her hair fell across his face, and he thought of the women before Lee Marie. He remembered sex when it was just sweat and heat. She rocked on his hips.

"Not in the car," he said.

"God," she said, and bit his cheek.

He flinched.

"Jesus," he said, and pushed her.

"I'm sorry," she said, and reached for his belt buckle.

It was imperative to clean the built-up glue from the Jumbo cutter blades, or the machine cut as if the rolls were no more than warm loaves of bread. Frost and Johnny watched each other's machines during breaks.

Frost returned with a bag of potato chips.

"They mine?" Johnny asked, staring. "Huh?"

"You're high," Frost said.

"I'll clean your machine, you give me those chips," Johnny said.

"You serious?" Frost asked.

"Am I what?" Johnny asked.

Frost looked around. "High?"

"I lost my job for shit like that," Johnny said. "You want your machine clean or what?"

A tube of uncut tape fed into the rear of the Jumbo as the front door closed and the safety bar descended. When the bar lifted, a dozen individual rolls slid forward onto a conveyor line.

"Cuts like butter," Frost said.

"Think I'm chicken? I'll do it with the blades running."

Frost tossed Johnny the chips. "You don't have to do nothing stupid."

Johnny caught them one-handed, but he no longer cared. He tapped his finger in the center of his chest. "If Johnny Cast says he'll do it, then he does it good."

"Right," Frost said, but he knew Johnny wasn't finished. Johnny wasn't the type. Izzy had told stories about Johnny in high school, how Johnny had smoked his first joint and vowed to be the biggest druggie in school and how after reading a chapter in the Bible, while flying on 500 mics of mescaline, he had zeroed in on reinventing himself as a Born Again, which lasted until he enlisted. It was all a great big competition.

"Take it easy," Frost said.

"How about you tell me who the father is if I reach in there?" Johnny asked. "I know she talks to you."

Frost held his hands in surrender. "It's not like that."

"I told her it ain't right to burden you with her problems."

"It's complicated," Frost said.

"You tell me who, and I'll cut that fucker in half with a sword," Johnny said. "I swear to God."

He rolled one sleeve to his elbow.

The safety bar dropped, and the machine sectioned another tube.

When the bar rose, Johnny reached for the nearest blade, the teeth wrapped in warm glue. He shot in quick, like he was reaching into a lion's mouth. The safety bar dropped, and for a second Frost thought he was free, but Johnny stepped back hard, his arm pinched down, and the machine sliced it in two like it was held together by no more than strings. The safety bar rose, and Johnny spun on his heels, looking around without recognition. Blood spilled down the Jumbo's ramp and Johnny's body. *Gallons*, Frost would later think. He grabbed Johnny by the shirt to keep him from falling. Together they eased to the floor. Johnny's mouth opened and closed like a gasping fish.

"Christ, God, hold on," Frost said.

"Fucking bitch," was all Johnny said.

2:10 A.M. The sun would rise in a few hours, and if Frost left his stakeout for bed, Lee Marie would certainly wake.

They'd stare across crumpled sheets without a clue of what to say.

It had been two years since their first date in Kabul when they shared a pack of cigarettes and talked for hours about everything, a far cry from dinner two nights ago. Over microwave meatloaf, they had a fifteen-word conversation.

"Food's good," Frost had said.

"Didn't make it," Lee Marie said.

"It could be warmer," Frost said.

She sipped her beer and dabbed her mouth with a napkin.

"It's fine," he said.

He stabbed a square of meat with his fork.

"Too late for apologies," she said.

They were different people now, but neither one would say it.

Frost never told Lee Marie about his reoccurring dreams. For months, he dreamed of a girl from his ninth grade French class. Mandy Sobatka. He remembered the brown mole on her neck and the classroom discussions where she told him that she barrel raced at the rodeo. She felt like she was flying, riding her horse, Trigger, her red hair whipping. She spoke beautiful sentences, a few words English, a few en français. Frost told her that he'd never ridden a horse.

"It's like sex," she had said.

"Yeah, right," he said.

"But better," she said.

He recently found her again on the Internet. He told his neighbor, Bill. At the Chinese buffet, Bill joked that

Frost should start doing sit-ups if he planned on taking his clothes off.

Frost stopped short of telling Bill that he saw Mandy's photograph—the missing teeth and the scarf around her head to cover the bald patches.

"With Lee," Frost said, "nothing's spontaneous."

"You think your future's certain?" Bill asked.

In front of the sesame chicken, he waved the serving spoon.

"In last week's paper," Bill said, "there was an eighty-five-year-old down in Florida just swimming in the ocean, just treading water. Probably thinking of the chicks on the beach, I bet."

"A good life," Frost said, considering another piece of crab rangoon.

"And all the sudden, *wham*, a tiger shark up and kills him. Imagine that?"

Bill spooned sesame chicken onto his plate.

"Christ, nothing's certain," Bill said. "Nothing."

Then he dumped his chicken back into the pan.

Frost visited his father when he could. Abe complained about his hand mostly, phantom pain shooting through the missing pinky.

Abe sat at the kitchen table. The television broadcasted the local weather. Abe stretched his fingers, each knuckle naturally popping. Some bone song.

They played pinochle. Abe had forgotten the rules. Frost had watched as a boy when Abe played his mother. Frost remembered the way they looked at one another, or the way they refused to. They sat only a few feet apart. Abe could've reached up and brushed a crumb from her lip. But really, there may've been an ocean that separated them. Abe never had to tell her he was having an affair. She knew after her doctor informed her that there were reports of spontaneous resolution for Chlamydia.

It was the year that Abe met his second wife, Gina, in a bowling league.

NOT long ago, Lee Marie had asked Frost if he ever wanted to sleep with other women. Frost read the sports page. The Yankees had beaten Detroit, 11-6. Lee Marie poured a mug of coffee. Straight from the shower, her hair stuck together in thick strands like rope.

"Is this a joke?" Frost asked.

Lee Marie tasted her coffee spoon. "You wouldn't enjoy it?"

"Jesus," Frost said. "Are you asking permission to sleep around?"

"Don't make this about me," she said.

Frost thought of Bill's wife, Seline, and he thought of Izzy. Then he thought of Lee Marie with another man. He imagined her eyes closed and her lips parted. He thought she saw the worry on his face.

"This is ridiculous," he said.

"Fine," she said. "Don't lose your head."

4:30 A.M. Frost wasn't sure what he had expected—a gang of thugs? But the mailbox remained standing.

The refrigerator kicked on, and the noise startled him.

The motor had been on the fritz. He'd fix it one of these days. He heard squeaking in the bedroom, like bedsprings. Lee Marie had said she hears mice in the walls. But it was too steady, too calculated. He thought of Lee Marie touching herself. He wondered what she was thinking about. He almost called out. Instead, he slid his hand down his stomach, and he listened.

6:15 A.M. The sun climbed the eastern sky without worry or judgment.

Frost stared out the front window. He thought of how his father had said that every object has an opposite; some were clearly good and others bad. As a child, Frost asked which one the moon was.

"Depends," was all Abe had said.

They had split a can of beef stew for breakfast. The night before, Frost's mother had questioned Abe about her Chlamydia problem while she packed a travel bag.

"What's it depend on?" Frost had asked, eating a spoonful of stew.

Abe slammed both hands on the table.

"Depends if what you got is worth shining a fucking light on," he said. "Now don't ask stupid questions."

Frost stopped drawing circles in the notebook. He could see the word in his mind. It was on the tip of his tongue. He tried spelling it.

He wrote:

~~Azheimer's.~~

~~Olsheimer's.~~

~~Alzhymer's~~ Disease.

Frost imagined his father at the kitchen table with the toy pistol. Abe shuffled a deck of cards. He would deal to Gina. He held one perfectly shaped hand before him, proudly. His fingers pinched the bottom edges of the cards, showing how careful he could be, a tenderness to keep them from falling.

"Early onset Alzheimer's Disease," the doctors had said, "and it won't be easy."

Gina's dog, Missy, would settle against Abe's legs.

"Supposed to be a nice weekend," Gina would say.

Abe held the toy pistol, a finger on the trigger. Missy perked her ears, but Abe only patted her head. Frost imagined Missy's confusion.

"Maybe we can take a drive around the lake?" Abe would say. They could enjoy the autumn leaves, just the two of them, a reminder of the beginning—why they fell in love.

"We shouldn't make plans," Gina would say, and light a cigarette. "Something might come up."

"When did you start smoking?" Abe would ask.

"Years ago, dear. You got me started."

Abe would make a clicking sound from the corner of his mouth as if having a sudden recollection and lower his tired eyes. With one shaky hand, he would lay his cards, a spade flush, the only upper hand he could manage.

6:45 A.M. Frost watched the paperboy ride his mountain bike along the sidewalk. He was fourteen and his face shined with metal piercings. Frost had told Lee Marie that if he was their son, he wouldn't be allowed to leave the house like that.

"Don't start," Lee Marie had said, because they'd talked about children enough. Frost wanted a child; Lee Marie did not.

"I'm not arguing," Frost had said. "I'm saying that even after what happened to his sister, it's no excuse to look like that."

"Why would you say that?" Lee Marie asked.

A year ago, the boy's sixteen-year-old sister had gone missing. Frost never got the whole story.

The boy whipped newspapers at every door as if he was heaving fastballs. Frost imagined he heard each *thwaap*. The boy nailed Bill's truck, and the newspaper bounced into the bare spot where Seline always parked her Honda. The spot had been empty for weeks.

The paperboy stopped in the middle of the road, a newspaper and lighter in hand. He ignited a corner and opened the duct-taped mailbox, fanning the flames with the door, the wafting air aggravating the fire.

Frost's eyes darted to the Louisville Slugger.

Dummy, he thought. *He's only a kid.*

Flames spat from the vents, and the boy smirked as the smoke grew darker.

"Little fucker!" Frost yelled.

"I'm trying to sleep," Lee Marie called from the bedroom.

Frost grabbed the bat and slammed the door. He marched down the front steps. He pointed the bat at the boy, but the boy was looking away.

"Little shit-for-brains," Frost said.

"Fuck," the boy said, and kicked his leg over the bicycle, but his pant leg caught on the pedal.

Frost swung the bat hard at the back tire. The bike jerked forward, and the boy fell.

"I'll call the cops," the paperboy said.

"Call the cops!" Frost yelled. "They'll arrest you for knocking my mailbox down."

"It was a dare." The paperboy's leg was stuck beneath his bike.

"What did you say?" Frost cocked the bat to swing.

"A dare." The paperboy shielded his face with one arm, his body shaking. "It's always so fucked up, I just thought."

"You thought what?"

"I thought you were doing it on purpose. Like to be different."

"Who knocks his own mailbox down?" Frost asked.

"I don't know," the paperboy said, crying. "It seemed like art, or something."

Frost had seen actors on television and dead men piss their pants, scared men who had lost control of their bodies. This boy was scared to death, and Frost wanted him to piss himself.

"Get up," Frost said. "You're a mess."

He thought Lee was right. He'd be an awful father. But this was not his child. This boy was different; he earned this.

"Don't ever come near my fucking house again," Frost said.

The paperboy mounted his bicycle and sped off. But Frost knew his type. He would not listen—not to him, not to anyone.

7:00 A.M. The bedroom blinds were partially drawn. A slat of morning light stretched across the comforter. Frost undressed to lie down.

"I know who it is," he said. "The vandal."

Lee Marie breathed loudly.

"You up?" he asked.

"I'm sleeping," she said.

"It ain't completely broken," he said.

"Didn't you hear me?" she asked, and she rolled away.

He thought of the life they once had. But this was where they were now. Their rent was a month late. The water bill was forty days past due. The front lawn was a foot high, and the mower needed gas.

He closed his eyes.

He imagined driving to the gas station with the mower in the bed of his truck. At the pump, he'd read stickers that warned "Caution," "No Smoking," "No Open Flames." He'd quit, but he had loved to smoke. He thought it wouldn't kill him to start again.

Then he'd drive around the lake staring at the foliage, at all the flame-shaped leaves fluttering as the traffic sped by, and he'd think of his father. He'd brake the truck halfway across the Bachelorville Bridge and unhook the mower. He'd stand in the bed and look out over Sacandaga Lake. He and his father used to fish this lake catching walleye and northern pike. The blue sky was wide open above him, and he'd heave the mower as hard as he could. He'd watch the mower peak and fall to the surface of the lake, sinking seventy feet to the cold, murky bottom. *Home*, he'd think. And there it would rest with the ancient, rusted things.

DrugMoney

THE FIRST ROBBERY was fucking metal. All sharp edges and broken air. This Asheville winter night, heading to Beanstreets Coffee on the corner of Broadway. The Ford Escort pulled to the curb. Black and ruined, and hugging the concrete. I breathed a patch of air against the place where the airbags had exploded from the wheel long ago, now scarred with strips of duct tape. The patch of air hung like a fortune, and I was desperately trying to read it. Good or bad? Time would tell.

You're wondering why I drove to the coffee shop I worked at in the middle of the night to steal a few hundred bucks, right? On the surface, I had a good life. Rural kid with an education. Had a Psychology degree, even if it was mostly to understand my own head.

Now twenty-two and nothing to do. Wanted to be a writer, and everyone knows Southern literature is the best our country puts out. Like any craftsman, I needed to get trained by a master, so I moved to North Carolina to audit a class taught by Ron Rash.

I froze in the Escort. Waiting for some sign of life, some sign to tell me to go home. But a few seconds later, I was out the door.

"Never pull the emergency brake on this car," my dad used to say—because before the Escort was my car, it was his car. Salt from those winters in upstate New York rusted the cables, so if you pulled it, you'd lock it for good. Lived most of my life too afraid to err on the side of safety for fear of locking up too.

Gimme danger.

If life wasn't giving me the story I wanted to write, I'd fucking make it, I thought, and I conjured a story that would begin right now and end in El Salvador, to write about a long-ago war, and I was only a plane ticket away. All the greats wrote about war, and even if I never fought with the FMLN, I knew oppression. Every day I hit my forehead on the lowest bar people around me expected of a redneck kid. I could imagine that Salvadoran struggle, twenty years earlier, if I walked their jungles. That was where a few hundred dollars was going to take me. To the literary canon.

Squeezing my hands into fists, rocking my head back and forth like some pugilist, I wrapped my scarf around my face and locked the doors. Two a.m., and no one walked the sidewalks. But the cold air crawled over my skin, and something like panic tried to bore inside me. I wasn't a criminal, not like some people.

Pressed the coffee shop key into the lock and twisted.

Voila. Pushed the door shut behind me and opened the security box. Tiny red light flashing. When the red flashes, you get fifteen seconds to punch in the override code or a call goes to dispatch. How many seconds went by? Tapped number nine on the pad, but in the cold, I couldn't feel the button. A path for some writers was a war, but on the other hand, nowadays a good kid can throw his life sideways because he has a dumb urge and get sent to prison for something stupid and maybe write his all-American story there. It was a win-win, because writing a novel in prison was another way to get famous.

No more shaking; I hit nine, one, four, four, seven, and the red light turned green.

"What the fuck are you even doing?" that part of me still tethered to reason asked.

I had time to leave, lock the door, and get back in my car. Drive away and sleep in my bed and wake up and meet a nice girl and get married and work a steady job with a desk in an office and a chair that swivels and raises and lowers by pulling a lever and contribute biweekly to my 401k to retire fat and happy. I thought about all of this walking to the register.

Was I a good kid? Took my first communion at age seven, confirmed at sixteen. Worst thing I did in high school was get pulled over for speeding on my way to football practice. Senior year our team went undefeated, and everyone in town knew we were the best in the school's history, and maybe that would last twenty or thirty years. That time I got pulled over for speeding, though, Officer Bartone let me off with a warning and told me good luck at the big game. Maybe that was when I realized laws weren't really laws depending on who you were.

Under the register, in a cupboard without a door, was the infamous brown bag. Every day after work, the closing barista pulled the tens and twenties from the till. Some days $600 would be stuffed in the bag. Other days $1,200. Nothing logged on paper.

Richard, the owner, would come in the next day and grab the bag and take it home. But at night, the money just sat there. Waiting for Richard or me or somebody else to come and snag it.

In the nickel light of the bright night, I counted out a grand from the bag. Hot breath against my scarf until the fabric was wet; I tasted my bitter spit.

High beams streamed down the road. Was I ready for a cop to park, the officer to cup his hands to the cold pane? And when he saw me inside a dark shop, what would he say?

"Work the morning shift," I'd tell him. "Thought I'd get an early start."

"It's the middle of the night, son."

"Yep, the middle of the night," I'd repeat, because I had no alibi. "That's right. You got me."

And that's how our conversation would end, and he'd ask me to come with him.

How do you tell your aging mother you were arrested robbing a fucking coffee shop? Not even a bank. Bank heists had ruthless glamour. This was a chicken-shit robbery. How would I tell her the money was for a plane ticket to El Salvador, because I had a classmate who was obsessed with their decades-old civil war, and I couldn't think of my own story to write, so I stole his? How could she be proud of a plagiarist? A crook who steals ideas.

But the money was in the bag, and the car outside carried on down the road, lights like floating ghosts traveling somewhere, nowhere. Like me.

Pocketed $400, stuffing $600 back so no one would suspect anything. Set the door alarm and locked up in time for the security system to re-engage.

Green light, red light, good night, sleep tight.

Fuck, I was high. Not a drug in my system, but you could've fooled me. On the sidewalk, I couldn't feel my feet because they weren't even touching the ground. First, I floated three inches. And I was rising, like Jesus, but I grabbed ahold of a street sign and pulled myself back to earth. Gravity saved me from soaring into outer space, because I wasn't sure I'd ever get home. I had an imagination that would take me to Mars and every planet beyond that.

Pulled the scarf off my face, blowing a crystal ball of white air. The money bulged in my pocket, and I eased my foot off the brake, pushed the gas. A thousand pounds of metal propelled forward. From where I sat, I was only soft flesh and brittle bones, but I was alive. Energy screamed through me. And I read that patch of frozen air I breathed. It was a crystal ball, and it said tonight was a good night.

HEATHER, Heather, Heather. Imagine her. A fucking angel, right?

Heather played everyone's favorite records before anyone knew those bands. She showed up late and went straight to the system. Loaded a CD and cranked the dial. Blasted Spoon's *Kill the Moonlight*.

In the morning static at Beanstreets, before we opened for business, the first track's bleating keyboards broke the stillness like karate chops. Heather whipped her fried blonde hair. Danced like a puppet: arms at right angles and legs jumping.

"It shthould be louder, Teen Wolf," she said, through her lisp.

"It's good," I said, before grinding a pound of coffee.

"It's fucking great," she yelled, over the whir of crunching beans.

She called me Teen Wolf because of my beard; I called her Heather. We spent the morning cracking jokes, and we pulled espresso shots like I never robbed the shop. Like I wasn't chasing a future no one in my redneck town should ever chase because they all ended up at the same place—poisonously drunk with gout in their leg and leaning over the end of a counter at a dive bar in Nowhere, USA.

But when our shift ended, we wound up at Vincent's Ear. I liked Heather, but she looked like my cousin. Same nose. Never wanted to fuck my cousin, or Heather. Would've fucked her friend Liz, but Liz was a lesbian with armpit hair, which was sexy on Liz, but we were never going to happen.

We sat at the bar, and Heather offered me a piece of pink bubble gum.

"I'm good," I said, and asked the bartender for a coffee. He looked at me sideways.

"The coffee's shit here," Heather said, and the bartender agreed. Heather said, "Two milk stouts. Tastes amazing with gum."

I didn't want to drink-drink. The thing was, when I started, I wasn't going to stop until I was blackout. So, I forced myself to drink as slow as Heather, but then she sipped again, and I had to. And we ordered another beer in no time.

"I'm so pissed at Edwin," Heather said.

"Who's Edwin?"

"My boyfriend, dummy," she said. "Broke my phone last night. You know how many phones I've thrown at him?"

"Oh, what's-his-face, right," I said. "People only throw phones in movies."

"Five phones," she said, ignoring me. "I had a three-phone boyfriend once, but never a five-phone boyfriend."

"What'd what's-his-face do to deserve it?"

"What, are you writing a story, Sherlock?"

"If I wrote his story, it'd be the best damn story you ever read," I said. "But I got better stories to write."

"He's going to be famous. You could be the guy who knew him before all this. You know that? You want to write his biography?"

"Aren't you listening?" I asked.

"No one cares about books," she said. "Who do you think's more famous, Sherlock Holmes or Dr. Dre?"

"I'm going to write about guerilla wars and injustice and shit."

"Whatever," she said. "Five phones sounds like a lot when I say it, doesn't it? But I shouldn't drink so much, then I take it all out on him." She drank again and wiped her lips. "We might as well get two more, right?"

She broke the seal on a pack of Marb Lights.

"I'll take that gum now."

Heather lit a cigarette. Her face was puffy and red from drinking too much, and her skin was dented with acne scars and new zits shined, but she looked at me sideways, a good sideways, like a dopey puppy, and I thought, *I could kiss her.*

I had a brother at home, 1,500 miles away, who had gout and drank too much and was probably going to die of a stroke, and for as much as he didn't care when his last day would be, his condition made me think about my last day and how any minute could be my last minute.

"You're really pretty right now," I said.

"You think 'cause you're a writer, I'll fuck you?"

In all honesty, I think maybe I was trying to fuck her even though she looked like my cousin. But I was drunk, and she was pretty, and you'd be crazy to think there wasn't something between us.

"You deserve better than a rapper."

"No, I don't." She stared into the cloud of smoke. Another crystal ball floating, and she saw some good future. "But you're sweet to say so."

The bartender said, "You still want that coffee, man?"

"Just a shot of whiskey," I said.

"Two," Heather said.

We sat there and drank, and she smoked until we were good and drunk. What did it matter?

I wasn't a criminal even though I committed the crime. It was all drug money anyway because the owner of the coffee shop had a coke problem, and everyone knew he just took that money and snorted it all up his big fucking nose.

I robbed the coffee shop two more times. The second time for spending cash on the trip to El Salvador and the third because I was addicted to floating down the sidewalk, even though the last time was only a few millimeters. But then the funniest thing happened: someone else robbed it after me, and they got caught and took the fall for the whole thing.

See, I worked with some real pieces of shit. Not the baristas but everybody in the kitchen. Tim the line cook, Shelly the store manager. They both had serious problems. Met in a halfway house. Shelly was almost thirty, but she looked like she was pushing sixty. Skin all wrinkled, splotchy. She'd been arrested for possession of heroin, but she'd been sober for a year, and since she was the oldest employee, it was only natural Richard would make her store manager. Richard trusted her, and soon she hired Tim, who was a junkie and recently paroled. After our shift one day, Tim told me his whole story.

He smoked a cigarette too fast, but he did everything too fast. Walked too fast, talked too fast. Burned every bridge too fast. I wasn't going to be his friend, but he asked me if I wanted to grab a beer, and I knew he couldn't drink on account of the halfway house rules, but he said he'd watch me. I didn't have a problem with that.

Tim squinted one eye shut and pulled a deep drag. He

stank like fried potatoes from cooking home fries all morning, and his hair was greasy and spiked like a gutter punk.

"It wasn't really my fault," Tim was saying, as we walked to the bar. "But once you get started. See, me and my buddy weren't gonna smoke anything that night, but then we did, and it wasn't like we could just stop, so he's the one who wanted to just scare the old lady, and I was going to grab her purse and run off, you know, because she was old and couldn't catch me, but it all went to hell because, well. Have you smoked crank before? You see, when I grabbed her purse, she never let go, and I just kept yanking it until I was dragging her across the street, and people started looking, and she started screaming, so I hit her a couple times so she'd be quiet. You can hit an old lady pretty fucking hard, and I swear, she just wouldn't loosen up. I barely had no idea what I was even doing, but the funny thing is... she didn't have no money in her wallet. Nothing, and we go to jail, and now I got this record. For what? Not one dime out of it."

"Jesus," I said, imagining my own grandmother and some asshole being an asshole to her. "That's awful. I mean, horrible."

"Tell me about it," Tim said. "Would've been worth it for at least a hundred bucks."

A swell of horns thrummed from the speakers. Layered harmonies. Low and high vocals trying to stay in contact with the air. It felt good to start the workday with Heather. She looked at me and mouthed something. An idea, like a ghost. Had no idea what she was saying, but I knew all the basics. Could read it on her face, in her eyes. It wasn't good. We were lost souls, but for a little while we had each other.

"Richard's here," she said.

"Richard the owner?"

Richard was rail-thin, fifty something. Dyed black hair and eyebrows, constantly rubbing his nose. He was never around except Fridays when we got paid, but sometimes not until Monday if he didn't have money. But this was Wednesday.

"He wants to have a meeting," Heather said.

Trying to play it cool, I said, "What's the music?"

"New band from Montreal," she said. "They're called Arcade Fire."

"Sounds joyful."

"The album's called *Funeral*."

Richard pulled the staff together. Heather and me behind the counter, Tim stood cross-armed, and one of the other cooks sat on the couch.

"Are we all here?" Richard asked.

We nodded, uncertain.

"Okay, then," he continued. "You may've heard, but I had to fire Shelly. Now some of you were close with her, and she had a lot of potential, but as you know, Shelly had a history that I took a chance on and we came up short. We all did. Last night, there was a break in and as luck would have it, Asheville PD saw the light on at 2 a.m. so they stopped, and Shelly was here robbing the till."

"She had a rough life," Tim blurted.

"Now I'm not disputing that, but she did what she did, and there's no going back."

"Fuck you," Tim said, and took off his apron. "You got no idea what it's like."

"Okay, now," Richard said, trying to stay calm. "I know you two were close, so I'm going to let you vent right now."

Tim threw his cotton apron on the floor, like some grand gesture, but no one heard it land.

We all waited for what was next. For him to yell, "I quit." Or lash out worse. But instead, he walked out of the shop. Didn't slam the door, just the normal wooden clack as it closed. And then he was gone, and Richard said nothing of it. Like the entire scene was erased from history.

Then Richard continued, "Now I've had my suspicions for some time, but Shelly came clean about it all. It wasn't the first time, and she confessed she wasn't using it for drugs but to find her own apartment, and we just can't take chances on any more people with those types of problems."

"Is she in jail?" Heather asked.

"Look, I don't know what's going to happen to her," Richard said, "but I know that we got coffee to sell, and I don't want this to get in the way, so how about we all just move on. Sound like a plan?"

Everyone in that room should've seen the sweat on my face. I've seen guilty people before, and I would've spotted me in two seconds. My heart was dropkicking my chest, and it took everything to only shrug and say, "Sure."

"You're all a good group," Richard said. "A great group,

and I'm lucky to have you here. So, let's have a great day. Okeydokey?"

Heather looked at me. "You okay?"

"Huh?" I said.

"Pretty heavy," she said. "You wanna pick the next CD?"

"*Funeral*'s good for me."

DRUGMONEY was Asheville's answer to the White Stripes. But they never got famous. The singer, a longhaired dreamer named Fisher, hung out at Vincent's Ear most days and played on stage most nights.

I'd been drinking since the shift ended. Heather had come and gone. She needed to buy another phone. It was going on midnight when Fisher and his drummer walked across the stage. He picked up his guitar and with it, he made a sound like a UFO landing.

I stomped my feet, head rocking back and forth, but gravity wasn't working for me. I wasn't sure I could stay upright, so I freed myself of any extra weight, and chucked the can of Blue Ribbon as high into the air as possible. At that moment, I was pretty sure I threw it through the ceiling, and it kept going all the way to outer space. All black and stars and perfect. The first time I robbed the coffee shop, I had that feeling that I was heading into outer space, so I knew exactly where the can of Blue Ribbon was off to. And it was truly beautiful.

But today, I'd imagined my life in jail, serving a few years or whatever you get for robberies, and tonight was my release date.

Constant snarling drums and the droning guitar swirled around me and fifty other bodies. The room was an animal, and we were all organs, singing from the inside.

I wasn't sure if Ron Rash could ever teach me the sacred craft of writing like him. *But I made it out alive*, I thought.

I didn't believe in luck. Especially not retrospective luck. Whatever it was, though, I needed to take it seriously, because some day, some lonely cop was going to find me doing something I shouldn't be doing. Until then I'll wake up, and I'll try to do better. I'm nearly positive that can of Blue Ribbon never fell back to earth. And if it could fly away, so could I.

Good Night

COLD AND WINTER. The land frozen. Evening air carved through each breath I took. Down the logging road, I saw the bend where it disappeared. The forest was cloudy and colored in dark shades I could not call by name, and black outlines of sugar maples and white pines were painted against the ground. With the sun slanted off to the west, only a thin glow grazed the canopy, a few pinpricks of light showing through to speckle the forest floor.

I exhaled and heaved wood into the bed of my father's pickup truck. Each chunk of wood that hit the bed shook flakes of rust onto the snowy ground. My father had cut and sectioned the trees much earlier but had forgotten about them, and since that time the pieces settled, the seasons moving around them, forcing the wood further and further into the earth.

Overnight a snowfall, dry and brittle, dusted the ground and hid the land once again. The logs meant nothing to my father, scattered about like rotting bird feed. I picked each log up, but he took no notice. Their sight no longer reminded him of the work he had done or that the staggering process was yet half over. The wood must still be retrieved and chopped and stacked and dried. In the end, however, it would be nothing but lost black cinders. The forgotten work of an aging man.

My muscles tightened and burned from the labor. I loved the heat. But soon the warmth was gone and my skin was wet and cold, my body less responsive. I struggled with the situation as he regarded me. He could be staring, but his eyes were unfocused. They were cracked into shards of white etched by thin red veins. And his skin was uncolored. He slapped his thumb against the butt of his cigarette, ashes flaring like fireworks as they fell and dissolved into nothing more than black crumbs on the snow. I could hardly see his gray eyes blending into the smoke before his face, and when the smoke lifted, he was staring and silent. The wind picked up, cutting through my jacket against my chest, and I shook with cold. Overhead, tree branches scraped against one another. I did not speak; instead, hunching over and hugging another log to pitch into the pickup. His face remained empty.

I stood for a moment, panting, waiting for my breath to slow. He continued to stare as if my face was something of a math equation, a language he could not read.

Tree branches fluttered as a cardinal perched among them. The blood-red feathers looked pasted onto the sky. I noticed nothing as brilliant as those colors. Dad pulled air hard into his lungs. He could not breathe deeply, and a low growl of a cough erupted from his gut and rose like a balloon to his lips. He spit a hack of red into the snow, the spot piercing the white layer. The heat in his phlegm melted the snow, slowly eating a hole three times the size of its entry, like cancer. The coughing fit convulsed through his body.

"About time I take a break," Dad said, huffing.

He had been watching me work for hours, shaking his head, his chin like a metronome.

I wished he would smile. I wished his stone face would break into something foreign but not painful. But he did not smile.

"Your mother'll probably have dinner about ready."

I looked at the knots protruding from the tree trunks. I looked at the glassy patches of snow, as perfect as mirrors. I looked at the face of my wristwatch. Both hands pointed to four. I had told him before, but he didn't care for what I had to say. We were done now.

I sat on the tailgate pulling off my gloves. They were stiff from the winter air. My hands were pink like a child's, blonde hairs matted flush. I heard the truck's engine start, and a puff of black smoke coughed from the pipes.

"You're not driving!" I shouted.

Dad sat in the driver's seat. He slowly drew his hands away from the wheel and stepped out of the cab. I walked around to the passenger side and opened the door to let him in.

As I drove down the potholed logging road, my body swayed absentmindedly. From the corner of my eye, I caught glimpses of trees bleeding into one another. I could not tell one from the next. I tried to give them meaning, but their blurred shapes meant nothing. Instead, I stared at the camouflage on my work gloves.

We came upon Dad's house. It stood, but that was all. It was nothing more than a ruin, a memory calling to be erased. Siding hung off here and there. He had tried to repair the damage over the years, but he was too far gone. Scraps of pine boards were hammered randomly onto the outer walls. There was no logic.

I fed the wood stove, and air as warm as bathwater washed through the home. I dipped a ladle into the crock-pot, spooning out venison stew. Hours earlier, I prepared the meal. I had cubed a flank of meat and chopped onions and potatoes and carrots. I handed him his share, and I sat across the table from him in the seat that he always took. Now he didn't care.

Inhumanly, he fed. He didn't blow on the stew. He spooned mouthfuls and dipped his fingers into the meal. He didn't rest until the bowl was clean.

"Your mother can still make a fine stew." He wrapped his tongue around each word, struggling to speak and swallow.

I knew what I had to say, what he needed to hear. But I paused because I had told him over and over again. Sometimes it was a day later or a week later, but no matter what, we both always came back to this.

"She's gone," I said.

"She'll be back." He was confident.

"She's been gone for twenty years," I said. "I'm all you got left, Pop."

He gazed, bewildered. He looked at me as if I was a stranger, hurtful. I tried to recapture the moment when I spotted the cardinal. The red bird was kind, but it was a wound against the sky. It would die someday, I knew that. But beautifully, I hoped.

And just as abruptly, his face was empty again, as if the passing moment had never occurred.

The kettle whistle still rang in my head like a mosquito hum. I poured boiling water into a mug full of coffee crystals. The night air was black and blanketed the house, and only the candlelight on the stove shone in the kitchen. The coffee was sour because nothing could be added; the milk he had forgotten about coagulated in the refrigerator. The candle flame fought as I breathed against it.

From the other room I heard him moaning, and I wandered to him in the dark. Through a window, a shave of moonlight covered half his back, and I could faintly make out the contours of his face.

"I'm sorry," he said.

"What?"

"I didn't mean to," he said. "It just, it just happened. It wasn't my fault."

"What's the matter?"

"My legs. They're numb. Sore from being here so long."

"Put your arms around me," I said. "I'll help you up."

"I can't," he said. "They left me. The women are gone. Your mother."

"You can't what?" I asked.

"Just let me, let me be." He swatted at my arms.

"Stop!" I said. "I'm going to help you."

"Why isn't she back yet?" he asked. "Where's your mother?"

"Let me help you up."

His words were confused as if he had been talking to someone else, somewhere else. He swung his head and raised his palm to slap me.

"Help? I don't need help," he said.

"Stop," I said, again. "You don't know what you're saying."

"You? Help me like you helped her? Where's she now? Had her goddamn hands on him like that. He was a boy, for Christ's sake. A goddamn boy."

I yanked him by his collar, but I knew I shouldn't have. He stared up, scared, like he would break into pieces. He had forgotten already. He reached for my wrists but began to tremble.

Dad tried to speak, but the sound of his words faded. I wrapped my arms around him and held him close.

"You're all wet," I said.

"My legs," he said, and stumbled. "They're sore."

"I'll take you to bed," I said. "Do you have to go again?"

"Put me to bed. I'm fine now. I'm fine."

"We should change your clothes."

"Put me to goddamn bed!"

I helped him into bed, but I did not pull the covers over him because he reeked of urine.

"Pull the sheets up!" he yelled. "Please."

His face looked yellow from the bedside lamp.

"Will you help me?" he asked.

I stripped the clothes from his body and dressed him in

a nightshirt. He didn't show any gesture or speak a word of appreciation.

"I'm alone now," he said.

"You're not," I said.

"I miss her."

"I know," I said, and I left the room.

The bathroom light was off; there was nothing to see. He had smashed the mirror in a fit that he could not remember. Hot water poured into my hands, and I washed my face. In my mind, I saw his eyes.

In the living room, I stared outside into the wilderness, but I could not see anything except the black sky and the slice of moon. The night air was cold, colder than that of the day, not because of the temperature but the emptiness. The unknown. The thought of ending at any moment—not only dying but being forgotten. I feared being crippled by recollections that would rot like apples over time. I thought of my daughter, Scarla. How long has it been? Six months? More? Night was colder for that reason.

I heard him again, shuffling around in his bedroom. I listened and imagined him dancing. I saw his face shining, grinning. I heard him crooning. Soft and colorful. For the past months that I had cared for him, I thought I could make him better. But now I know it will only get worse.

"Are you okay?"

I waited, but there was no response.

"I'm coming," I said. "I'll be right there."

I pushed the bedroom door open, and he was curled on the floor. He was not positioned like that because he wanted to, but because he felt he had to. Every night I found him in the same claw-like position. He said the hardness hurt, which reminded him he was still alive. But he was not. He was dead inside, and he woke every morning with hardly a memory of the last night.

He mumbled, but I couldn't hear the words or make sense of those I did.

"Your mother and me. We were children. Not weak. Wasn't like that. We worked, worked hard. We were children when this country was, when your name meant something. It means something, doesn't it?"

He remained coiled on the floor and continued talking, but his words drifted further away.

"Where is she?" he asked. "Don't let her go, son. If she runs again, she won't come back. Not ever."

As a boy, I too had run away, needing to prove I could take care of myself. But I could not, and he knew this. Through most of my teenage years we'd never spoken a word of it. It was only when I was seventeen, before leaving for good, that he had told me. He said that he had something to give me, and I figured he would hit me, tell me I was being stupid, tell me that the world would eat me alive. He would say that no good man runs from trouble, and I could picture his mouth, dark and vile, telling me how I should live my life. It seemed we never had anything in common because all we shared was a last name. But he knew exactly why I had to go.

When we met, he handed me an envelope, and I remembered his face. He was young and still cared for life. His eyes were bright, and his face flushed pink.

"What's this?" I had asked.

"I could never say it," he said.

"Say what?"

"Not like it wasn't there," he said. "Was always there."

I rubbed my thumb across the letter's edge.

"Even without your mother, I tried my best," he said. "I know she left because of me. I take responsibility. But I swore I'd always do right by you. Try to remember that."

I had forgotten that letter—his words of love.

DAD laid his head back onto the bedroom floor, but I lifted him into my arms. He was weightless, as if only a breath of air. I rested him in bed and pulled the sheets and blankets close to his chin, tucking him in like a child. His breath was warm and even, and I pressed my palm against his forehead.

"It's fine now," I said. "Everything will be okay."

The next morning I would learn it was the coldest night on record, but now his eyes opened. They were a bright season. I leaned to him, kissing his nose. Good night.

Trip the Light Fantastic

"Pussy cum," she said.

We examined the flakey stain on the corner of the duvet. Since we arrived at the Airbnb house first, I convinced my girlfriend it would help her sleep better if we snagged the biggest room. She almost said yes until she saw the stain.

"I'm definitely not sleeping here," Hazel said.

"It's crusty detergent," I said.

But I stripped the bed, and the mood changed. We stretched out to nap and thinking about a stranger cumming hard made me hard. My fingers enjoyed a ten-second slide up Hazel's body, and I pinched her nipple, the flesh straightening, and she closed her eyes. I squirmed down the mattress and spread her legs and licked her. When I gazed up, she was staring out the window, no longer in the room but someplace in her mind. I stopped, but she seemed not to notice.

I rolled over, and she said, "Are you mad or something?"

"You didn't seem very interested," I said.

"It's going to be a long night," she said. "I just thought we were going to take a little nap."

"We have this entire house," I said. "And no one else is even here yet. But if you're tired, you're tired. I get it."

She angled her face toward mine, grinning sheepishly, and she reached between my legs, stroking me. Then she anchored over my hips, guiding me inside of her.

WE were an hour east of Portland, in Hood River. Everyone else arrived after dinner, five of us, and no one was shy about tomorrow's wedding. We were the second wave of invitations—the pity party. Was anyone's name even spelled right on the cards?

After a few vodkas, Maurice said that Avery had brought a special treat, and the waffle maker at the Airbnb was as good as any sink in a public bathroom to snort coke.

Maurice cut five lines; it wasn't his first time.

"Lick the edge of the card," Maurice said, holding a black credit card to my lips.

Zee edge, he really said, like a cartoon, and I loved everything about him: his tight denim shorts, his black-rimmed glasses, and his wife Avery. *Who could ever cheat on her?* I thought, as I dragged my tongue like a dog across the plastic.

I saw Avery naked twice that night.

The first time was an hour later. She stood in the corner of the living room, her porcelain back to us as she shimmied into dress after dress. Maurice scrolled through pictures on his iPhone and Hazel was half-asleep on the couch, hugging her knees to her chest, but Ronni and I were watching Avery.

"I'm so stressed about this," Avery said, and she let her bra fall loose to the floor. She wore only a baby blue thong. But I couldn't enjoy anything because she was still complaining about the invitations. "I don't know. They probably just invited whoever would show up."

But the truth was, we'd been friends with the bride and groom for two years, and they were going to be 40-year-old newlyweds. *They waited long enough*, I thought.

MAURICE suggested a pick-me-up and cut five more lines. Our friend, Ronni, was in town from London. She produced a tiny glass straw from her purse.

"My roommate thinks I'm addicted," Ronni said, straw to her nose. "But I just like the way it smells."

Maurice recorded the scene on his iPhone.

"Don't show our faces," Avery said.

"We should play charades," Ronni said.

The first word was "Dragon Fruit," and Avery and I shouted out descriptions for Hazel.

I said, "A mythical beast that breathes fire."

Avery said, "The opposite of a vegetable."

Hazel shook her head, but then her eyes lit up. "Serrano pepper," she said.

"What?" I said, as our time ran out. "Why would you say that?"

"A hot vegetable," Hazel explained.

I had to wait another hour to see Avery naked again.

Hazel had retired to our room, and Ronni was jet-lagged and asleep on the love seat. The rest of us soaked in the hot tub on the deck. I was the only one wearing a bathing suit. Avery finally said she was pickled, and I turned politely away as she stepped from the water, wrapping a towel around her waist, and when I looked again she caught my eye, pausing too long before patting her bare chest dry and covering herself.

For a year and a half I've been trying to convince Hazel I'd marry her so she'd love me, but now nuptials were the furthest thing from my mind.

THAT night I had a dream about sucking my own cock. Hazel rubbed my back, encouraging me, as I gracefully tucked forward like a mother bird about to feed a chick, and I took the swollen glans into my mouth, circling the corona with my tongue. I didn't notice that we were in a public park until I felt a crowd of people closing upon us. I spotted a coworker among them, and I stopped, ashamed and embarrassed.

"There, there," Hazel said. "It's what you've always wanted."

THE morning of the wedding, I woke thirstier than I've ever felt. I thought about my dream. I knew I was going to marry Hazel someday, but I had no idea what would happen after that. I reached for the glass of water on the nightstand; the night-old water tasted like semen.

While everyone got ready, I returned to the Jacuzzi. Dead insects floated in the still water. I only planned to cover the tub, but I turned on the jets and the bubbles broke against the surface like boiling water and the dead insects bounced in the surf. I stripped naked and sat among them. They all boogied as if they returned to life for one final celebration. We all deserved that chance. Jesus, they danced.

Many thanks to the editors of the following journals, where earlier versions of these stories previously appeared:

- "Made by Brutal Beasts" in *Buckman Journal*
- "Home, Somewhere" in *Chicago Quarterly Review*
- "Baby Teeth" and "Descendants of the Crow" in *BULL: Men's Fiction*
- "Masters of Matchsticks" in *SmokeLong Quarterly*
- "American Metal" in *Baltimore Review*
- "Other Animals" and "Trip the Light Fantastic" in *Hobart*
- "Last Days at Wolfjaw" in *Tin House*
- "Sky Meets Sea" in *Juked*
- "About Future" in *Fiction Southeast*
- "Modern Lovers" in *Nervous Breakdown*
- "Dracula Mountain" in *CutBank*
- "Saturday Night Special" in *Carbon Copy Magazine*
- "Good Night" in *Puerto del Sol*